MURDER AT THE MARINA

A ROSE BLAIR MURDER MYSTERY

JUDY KEIGHTLEY

ISBN-13: (Paperback) –978-0-9919187-3-7
Publisher: Judith Keightley

To My Family
This one is for Dean,
my latest fan

ACKNOWLEDGMENTS

Any errors and omissions of an historical or factual nature are mine and for this, I humbly apologise.

I would like to thank my dear friends who read and edited, namely Kate and Margo.

A huge thank you to Laura Gruer, our darling daughter, who spent much time designing the book cover while tending to baby Tabitha!

Also, as usual I owe a huge debt of gratitude to my husband Philip, for his support and patience during the process of writing and editing this, my fourth Rose Blair Murder Mystery novel.

PROLOGUE

Rose looked around and realized that she was the only person down by the docks and something about that made her feel distinctly uncomfortable. The marina was very quiet which she supposed wasn't surprising as it was still very early on in the season, and it was also mid-week.

She carried her cleaning materials onto the jetty beside their boat, *Tranquility*. The plan was to give the boat a good 'spring clean' before Tom started the sailing season again.

Rose stepped onto the boat and was just about to unlock the cabin, when she heard the insistent thud, the thud of something bumping up against the side of the boat. She looked over the starboard side into the space between *Tranquility* and her neighbour's boat. There, caught between the buffers of both boats, was the body of a woman floating face down in the murky water...

ONE

SAFARI

Tom didn't do surprises. In all the years that they had been married, Rose had never known Tom to be spontaneous. She loved him to pieces, but predictability was one sure fact about her husband. It was, therefore, an amazing surprise when, last September at her birthday party, Tom had presented her with two air tickets for an African safari. They would leave the following March, flying to Kenya, and spend one week on safari and then one week at an East African beach resort on the coast of the Indian Ocean.

That had all been and gone, and already Rose was finding it difficult to recall the names of the other people on the safari. She picked up the photo album that Tom had put together of their trip and flipped through. As her eyes rested on the group photo of all six couples, she smiled to herself. Although it was a cliché, their holiday had truly been a holiday of a lifetime.

Right from the onset when they had arrived at Nairobi airport, having left Toronto in a blizzard, their eyes had never stopped blinking in amazement at the sights before them. Africa had shocked their senses into overdrive. Everything was so different from Canada, and they had loved every bit of it.

The other five couples on the safari were introduced to Rose and Tom at the New Stanley Hotel, which was situated in the middle of the crazy busy city of Nairobi. There was Pete from Berkshire, England. He was a retired accountant from Reading and his petite wife Carol, was a retired nurse. The safari was a retirement present from their children.

Jan and Andre were from Windhoek in Southwest Africa. They had already been on several safaris, but all in South Africa. They were a little younger than Rose and Tom. Andre was a big bear of a man with thick, black curly hair and a beard. He had warm, friendly brown eyes that looked a bit like a Spaniel's. Jan, on the other hand, was quite petite and had fine, blonde hair cut into a bob and streaked with blonde highlights. She looked almost Nordic with her piercing blue eyes and high cheek bones and was very attractive wearing designer clothing, which Rose noticed straight away. They immediately struck up a friendship with each other vowing to stay in touch after the safari was over.

Doug and Polly were from Hampshire, England, and both were retired teachers. Doug had shocking white hair and awfully gappy teeth. He smoked like a chimney and was always cracking raucous jokes which Rose wasn't sure how to take, but he and Tom got along really well. His wife, Polly, barely said a word. She was pleasant enough and joined in with everything, but the word 'mousy' came to mind when Rose thought of her. Doug and Tom shared a beer together on more than one occasion and when Polly was asked if she would like to join them at the bar she always refused, making Rose feel awkward if she wanted to be with Tom. Doug and Tom shared the same sense of humour and spent most evenings laughing away at old jokes.

Then there was the young couple, Linda and John, who were

on their honeymoon. They were so wrapped up with each other that they barely mingled with the rest of the group, going off to their beds long before anyone else. Rose smiled while remembering some of the sounds coming from within their tent.

The last couple, Baptiste and Juliette, were from Normandy in France and, although they spoke very good English, kept to themselves. Baptiste was a potter, and he looked a bit like an ancient hippie with long flowing shoulder length hair and irregular teeth that seemed to overcrowd his mouth. Juliette was a doctor and had worked for years with Médecins Sans Frontieres.

Whereas Baptiste was wild and free spirited, Juliette appeared to be the polar opposite. She was very tidily dressed in crisp, khaki shorts and pearly white cotton shirts and always wore a black head band to tie her long hair back off her face. They were not exactly unfriendly, but aloof was probably more the word to describe them. Rose had tried to hold a conversation with Juliette when she found out that she was a doctor with Médecins Sans Frontieres, Rose had been both impressed and interested to hear which countries she had worked in, but it seemed that Juliette did not want to talk about her work and had all but snubbed Rose.

Their orientation had taken place the day after their arrival and was conducted out on the hotel's terrace overlooking the swimming pool. They were to travel in two separate canvas topped Land Rovers. The first base camp was 12 km into the Masai Mara game reserve.

They had left Nairobi that same morning and had initially travelled on an impressive newly paved highway which soon gave way to a rutted, potholed dusty road with just a strip of tarmac in the middle. Rose remembered being jolted on the hard back seat of the Land Rover. Several times she had clung to Tom for fear of actually being bounced out of the open sided vehicle. The entrance to the game reserve had been exciting as a whole troop of baboons had camped by the wooden gates and, even though the driver had honked on his horn, the baboons had refused to leave their post until a bunch of bananas had been thrown to them. This, apparently, was such a regular occurrence that the drivers had taken to carrying bananas in their vehicles.

Rose remembered their first impression of the Masai Mara Lodge. The lodge was nestled in a clearing by the side of a small river. There were eight rondavels, little round huts with conical thatched roofs dotted all around the perimeter with one larger thatched building, in the middle. Stones painted white formed the edge to graveled pathways connecting the small cottages to the main lodge.

Everywhere Rose and Tom looked they could see a riot of colour, with lots of crimson red bougainvillea bushes as well as dahlias and zinnias of orange and gold, planted in flower beds around Frangipani trees, sweet in their fragrance and laden with waxy-white flowers growing from silver branches.

Around the perimeter of the lodge, majestic Jacaranda trees grew smothered in tiny bluebell-like flowers which formed a colourful blue carpet at the base of each tree. Honeysuckle tumbled over the entranceway to the lodge which, once inside, was all wooden panels and floors with floor to ceiling glass windows overlooking the slightly muddy looking river. Zebra and springbok skins were scattered over the floors. There were small round tables and chairs made from rattan and a bamboo bar.

Visitors to the lodge could watch the hippo's wallowing in the mud by the side of the river, and if they waited long enough the odd crocodile would appear. Springboks, zebras, and lions regularly visited the river always with whole troops of baboons that seemed to have taken over the place. Their tour guide had warned them all never to feed any of the animals, particularly the baboons who had come to expect human food and were beginning to demand it.

Rose was a bit fearful of the baboons with their patchy, wiry short haired coats. She noticed that they all had very long, sharp yellowed teeth and fingernails, and their bright orange knobby bottoms looked suitably ugly. But it was their faces that perturbed Rose the most. Their clear, dark brown, shiny, beady, and intelligent eyes always looked cruel and calculating to Rose.

Their guides had also warned them about walking around in the dark. In Kenya daylight went from being light to dark almost instantly, like turning off a light switch. Leopards particularly liked to hunt at night and although the lodge had its own watchmen, sometimes a leopard had been known to creep into the fold and cause havoc, mostly with the chickens the cook kept for his kitchen. Rose and Tom had no intention of going anywhere at night although there was a night-time safari tour on offer, which they could take if they wanted.

Their rondavel huts were spotlessly clean with ceramic floors and whitewashed walls. They had their own toilet and wash basins inside, but all the showers were outside on a small, screened patio. The bedcovers and furniture were all white. A huge wooden bowl laden with tropical fruit sat on a small coffee table situated between two soft, white easy chairs. A vase of bright red cannon lilies sat on the dressing table next to a bottle of wine in an ice bucket with two wine glasses. On each pillow lay a silk pouch with Amarula liquor truffles nestled inside. The whole room was enchanting, and Rose loved it.

That first night at Masai Mara Lodge, Tom and Rose made love to the sounds of lions roaring and a whole cacophony of noises, as nocturnal animals padded past their window preparing to hunt for the night. Rose felt that she was on another planet - it was all so different and magical.

Another photograph in the album caught her attention. It was of Andre and Tom standing arm in arm with huge smiles on their faces. There was the watering hole in the background with a whole herd of elephants of all shapes and sizes in and out of the water. The whole memory of their elephant adventure came flooding back to Rose as if it was yesterday.

The "Night Safari' and the "Sunrise with Elephants" had been two of the extra packages included in the safari. Tom and Rose had opted for the elephant tour even though it had meant getting up at 4:00 a.m. Jan Du Preez had cried off claiming that she definitely was not a morning person and needed her beauty sleep.

They had all tumbled out of bed in the pitch darkness of night which had made Rose feel very nervous as in her mind those nocturnal leopards could still be out scavenging for the cook's chickens or worse. But Tom urged her to ignore all thoughts of big cats and soon they were safely aboard the open topped Land Rover and bumping along the rutted road. Daylight slowly crept in and the whole landscape was eerily bathed in grey and pink light.

The watering hole most commonly used by the reserve's herd of elephants was situated 30 kilometres from the lodge. The drive was magical as everything looked so different in the early morning light. Trees appeared like skeletons and there was something almost spooky about the mist rising from the ground in thin, whispery bands. It reminded Rose of a staged Halloween pageant. All they needed were a few witches and ghosts to appear to set the scene perfectly.

They arrived at the watering hole just as the sun rose. It was a truly spectacular site. The enormous red disc lined in purple streaks with pink, marshmallow clouds surrounding the whole sky.

The Land Rover driver parked under a giant baobab tree, and they all jumped out, although Tom helped Rose who was nervous about the jump down. Their guide beckoned for them to follow him. Once again Rose felt extremely apprehensive as there were shadows everywhere and strange noises pierced the night. She half expected a lion or leopard to leap out at the group at any moment.

The guide set up "camp" behind a large thorn bush and the first thing he did was warn the group to be on the lookout for snakes. The puff-adders were the worst as they were traditionally lazy and liked to bask in the sunshine. Many a traveler had accidentally stepped on these snakes and had not lived to tell the tale. It was not sunny yet, thought Rose, while carefully watching where she stepped. She did, however, wonder where those sun loving snakes slept at night.

The guide had chosen an excellent view of the muddy drinking hole for the elephants. The wait seemed like forever, but it was about twenty minutes before the first giant elephant appeared. He was a bull, one of the male elephants with tusks almost five feet in length. The guide explained that poachers still killed the elephants for their tusks, although Masai Mara Game Reserve had not had an incident of poaching for the past two years.

The grey shapes started moving towards the water like huge rocks in a steady stream. At first count Rose and Tom saw twelve fully grown elephants with three babies trailing along. How they didn't get trampled by the mammoth adults was beyond Rose.

Slowly, one by one, they filed down to the water where they proceeded to wade into the muddy water, then the fun began. It was like children playing at the seaside, trunks in the water, spraying each other playfully, swishing their trunks and tails, submerging their giant bodies, and coming up to a spray of water. They really did look as if they were enjoying themselves, even the babies joined in the fun.

There was one incident that frightened Rose and that was

when two bull elephants started to butt each other aggressively with their giant tusks. It looked as if they were truly going to kill each other. The fight lasted all of five minutes, and it was difficult to tell who was victorious as both bulls walked away in opposite directions swinging their trunks, flapping their ears, and flicking their tails while shaking their whole head. *They were probably fighting over another female elephant,* Rose thought, *it was always about sex in the end.*

The tour concluded with a photo opportunity whereby the guide grouped everyone together with the elephants in the background. Rose then took a photo of just Tom and Andre standing arm in arm, looking so relaxed and happy that she was filled with a huge sense of gratitude. This rough, rugged African landscape appealed hugely to Tom. *He should have been born in Africa,* she thought, just like Andre.

Glancing at the photo album, again Rose smiled at the photograph of Tom, Andre, and Jan standing next to a cheetah cub called Uhuru. The cub had been found next to his mother who had been shot by a poacher.

Christopher, the Masari Lodge manager, had personally raised the young cub and now, at six months, he was as tame as any puppy dog and just as friendly. He would, in time, grow too big to handle and then they would start a program of rehabilitation, but until then, the guests at the lodge loved the opportunity to pet the young cub. In the photograph, Jan had her arms draped around 'Uhuru' while Andre, had his arms draped around her shoulders. Tom stood slightly to one side smiling at the camera. *They all looked so happy,* Rose thought.

With that last thought Rose closed the album and let out a big sigh. She glanced at her watch. It was ten o'clock, Tom would be back from pole-walking, and she would have to get her skates on if she was to bake the scones she had intended to bring around to her friend Susan Parker's house. She pulled out the ingredients, turned on the oven, and proceeded to make Susan's favourite orange and cranberry scones.

Susan. Every time Rose thought about her friend her heart gave a little lurch. She had gone through so much and her pain had been so palpable that Rose had not known how to help. The only thing that she could do was to be there for her, that and to cook.

When Susan was still living in London, Rose had driven over once or twice a week carrying casseroles and cakes, scones, and bottles of wine which they had both consumed over teary recollections of how life could have been with Henri Le Bruin had he not been killed in action the previous year. Susan and Henri were to be married having finally reconciled that one of them would have to move.

It had been Susan's decision to sell her darling cottage in London and move to Montreal where they would buy a home together. All those plans had changed in an instant on that one fateful day when Henri had been shot by Jim Reynolds at Centralia Airport.

Following the incident Susan had fallen into a massive depression, so much so that for months afterwards she had been unable to work, and last September she had finally handed in her notice.

After thirty years on the police force, Detective Inspector Susan Parker had retired, sold her house in London, and bought a condo in Harbour Court, Bayfield.

Now, almost nine months later, Rose's old friend was finally emerging from her cocoon-like state and had almost regained her previous 'joie de vivre.' She no longer looked gaunt and haggard. Her thick, chestnut coloured hair now glistened with health and renewed vitality, as did her eyes.

She had gained a bit of weight and had started dressing better. For the previous nine months Rose had only seen her friend wearing tatty t-shirts and jeans. The smart, elegant career woman had disappeared, only to be replaced with a lackluster, hollowed eyed shadow of the woman Rose had known. *Shock and trauma could do that to you,* Rose thought for the hundredth time, shock and grief at the loss of a loved one.

With the scones in the oven, Rose opened the back door and let Ben and Puff, her beloved dogs, outside. It was a beautiful day with not a single cloud in the turquoise blue sky. She could hear the birds singing. One particular song trilled out the loudest and Rose looked out to see where it was coming from. There, perched on one of the thin branches of the pear tree was a little red breasted robin singing its little heart out. Ben and Puff charged out into the garden and the small bird flew away. Rose decided to leave the dogs outside. Tom would be home within the hour, and it would be good for them to have some fresh air.

Rose gathered up the still warm scones and grabbed her car keys. She was about to leave when, on second thought, she stopped and found a scrap of paper to write a note for Tom telling him that she had gone to Susan's for coffee and that she would be back at lunch time. She had already told Tom her plans for the day, but he had been busy reading the newspaper and she wondered just how much he had taken in. Tom suffered from a form of 'deafness' called 'selective hearing' and it drove Rose crazy.

After lunch she had told Tom that she would go down to their boat, Tranquility, and give it a much needed clean. It had only been put back into the water a week and still had all the winter cobwebs and dust inside. Tom still had varnishing and some minor body work to complete, but the boating season had just begun.

Rose had just closed the front door and was about to jump in the car when she heard the telephone ring. Quickly opening the door and retracing her steps back to the kitchen, she grabbed the phone. There was total silence on the other end and then the broken ring tone as the phone was disconnected.

Someone had obviously dialed the wrong number, Rose thought as she once more walked out to the car and prepared to visit Susan, her friend.

TWO

Susan loved living in her comfortable condo on Harbour Court. There was a swimming pool on the grounds although it was still too cold to use just yet.

The new owners of The Ashwood Inn, formerly The Bayfield Village Inn, had said that Susan could use their indoor pool anytime, but although the offer was tempting, she could not bring herself to step foot inside the Inn. There were too many memories of Henri and her associated with the old Bayfield Village Inn, and she did not want to risk opening up her still tender heart to those poignant reminders of days past.

Rose's visits were always something to look forward to, particularly as she never came empty handed. It was her friend's cooking that had sustained Susan all through those darkest hours of her despair.

Thinking back forty years, she remembered how Rose had always been the nurturer. At Queen's University, where both had studied, she would bake brownies and regularly made pancakes for all the girls who shared the dormitory.

Susan had then been the party girl, the wild child, and Rose was the very opposite. It was not at all surprising that Susan had ended up marrying a 'jerk' and was divorced within three years, whereas Rose had married her childhood sweetheart, and they had been now together for over forty years.

Susan had embraced her career and had climbed her way up the predominantly male oriented ladder of the police force. She still missed the adrenaline rush that every new case brought in and she missed the camaraderie, but she loved living in the village of Bayfield and was determined to make it truly her home.

Rose's visit went well with the two women chatting away amicably. Inevitably the conversation got around to the present diet Rose was on and how much longer she would stay with that particular one. Susan always looked at her friend Rose and marveled at how she could gain weight and then could lose it, up and down like a yoyo. She had spoken to Rose about the bad effects of dieting and Rose had nodded and said that she knew dieting was bad and she was eating very well, but the weight seemed to come out of thin air, and it was an awful curse.

Rose, on the other hand, looked at her friend Susan and thought to herself that slim people would never be able to understand the hardships of suffering from a sluggish metabolism. She had only to eat one piece of cake and it was as though it instantly turned to fat in her legs.

"Susan," Rose said changing the subject somewhat, "Why don't you join the Croquet Club? We have the opening season cocktail party coming up and new members are welcome. You could join Tom and I and meet some of the members, they're a great crowd."

"I might just do that, Rose. It is about time that I became more social. What time and where is it to be held?"

"It's at 5:00 p.m. this Saturday at the Town Hall."

At the mention of the Town Hall Susan's face dropped. It had been during the murder at the Town Hall investigation that Henri had been shot, although his murder was not at all related to that particular inquiry. Susan hadn't set foot in the Hall since the previous year. Just like the Village Inn, some places had become taboo to her as they carried the ghosts of the past.

Rose understood Susan's dilemma and that only time would heal her fears. She would not push her friend, although she knew that the Croquet Club would be a perfect place for her to meet some new people.

It was time to leave, and Rose got up to hug Susan.

"Paul, Jessica, Rob, and the girls are coming over this Sunday for lunch. Why don't you join us as Tom fancies doing a barbeque? He's dying to try out our new grill. Please come. Abby and Ella will love to see you again."

Susan thanked Rose and smiled, saying, "Oh, Rose, where would I be without you."

Rose returned to their Bayfield Terrace home in a happy mood. As she parked, she felt her heart lift with joy. She loved their house, and with summer in the air everything was waking up after the long winter. The climbing rose over their front porch already had buds just waiting to burst open and the honeysuckle too. This year Tom had put in a raised vegetable garden in the back yard in between the pear and apple trees. Rose was anxious to plant the tomatoes, but Tom kept reminding her that they should wait until the end of the month for fear of a late frost.

As she walked into the lobby, the first thing she noticed was the absence of the dogs greeting her. The house seemed silent and unwelcoming without the normal barking and wagging of tails she was used to. *Tom must have taken them for a walk*, Rose thought as she walked into the kitchen, but no, she heard barking coming from the back door. Puff and Ben were still outside, which could only mean one thing and that was Tom hadn't been home. Rose let the frantic dogs in and after fussing over them she noticed Tom's handwriting scrawled across the note that she had left for him earlier.

"Playing golf with Doug."

Rose sighed. He must have come in from pole walking and literally gone straight out again with Doug unaware that Puff and Ben were outside. *Oh well, no harm had been done,* she thought, while opening the fridge and pulling out the makings of a salad.

Tom had obviously been to their post box as a pile of mail sat on the counter. Rose flicked through the post absentmindedly. There were mostly flyers, but sandwiched between a Rona and a Canadian Tire leaflet was a postcard. It featured the Statue of Liberty in the centre with shots of Time Square, Central Park, the Rockefeller Centre, Ellis Island, and the Brooklyn Bridge. Rose turned the card over and read the few words written on the back, scanning down to the bottom to see who the card was from. It was from Jan and Andre, their friends from South Africa whom they had met on the safari a couple of months ago.

Rose now remembered them saying that they were going to be touring America in May and visiting their daughter who lived in New York. The card had been mailed ten days ago. Jan had written that Andre and she were renting a car and would be driving up to Canada to visit them. Rose gave a start. Jan and Andre could be arriving any day now, and she then immediately thought of the upcoming weekend when the family were due to visit.

That would be nine people to cook for which didn't bother her, but she just wanted to make sure that there would be enough food if they were to have two extra guests. Jan was a vegetarian too so that would add to the planning and preparation. Somoza came to mind, an Indian Dahl too, as Jan loved Indian food. *How exciting,* Rose thought, *to be seeing Jan and Andre again. What an unexpected pleasure.*

It was two o'clock before Rose finally grabbed a bucket, dusters, and cleaning material to take down to the marina. She was just about to leave the house when the telephone rang. Rose grabbed the phone having ran to get it in time and was thoroughly fed up when all she got was silence at the other end of the line. *It was probably a wrong number,* she thought as she closed the front door and walked towards her car.

The marina was very quiet which wasn't surprising as it still was very early in the season. In fact, Rose realized that she was the only person around. She parked her car in the small parking area next to the Cottage Colony. Rose looked down the line of slips.

Tranquility, Tom's beloved boat, was docked alongside six other boats all about the same size. The boat was really Tom's baby, and even though Rose sailed every now and then with him she wasn't so keen. Not all the boaters had put their boats in the water, yet certainly by the end of the month every slip would be taken and the whole marina would be in business again for the summer season.

But for now, it was eerily quiet, and Rose dwelt on the fact that a hundred years ago the harbour would have been teaming with fishing boats. What most people had forgotten was that the community around Bayfield had been built up on the fishing industry which had brought in herring, white fish, salmon, and trout.

In the springtime most of the fishermen had fished for perch and there had been at least two dozen fishing boats regularly moored at the same slips where Rose now stood.

She remembered a talk that Tom and she had attended at the Historical Society. It had been all about the fishermen of Port Bayfield. Hughie Macleod was talked about with great affection as he had been one of Bayfield's more colourful characters. He liked his liquor and could tell a tale or two. Hughie had also built boats one of which he had named after his deceased baby daughter, Helen Macleod. It currently was in the process of being restored by the Historical Society and was the only fishing boat of its kind left in Ontario.

Bayfield fish had been mostly shipped to America to Detroit, Chicago, and New York. Fresh water mussel shells were also exported to make buttons. Rose recalled the great storms that had hit Lake Huron and the many tragedies attributed to the lake. The biggest storm of the previous century had taken place in November 1913.

For four days there had been blinding rain, hail, sleet, and hurricane force winds. Nineteen vessels went down to a watery grave and over two hundred and forty bodies had been washed up and found strewn along the beaches. Rose remembered how four years ago one of the missing cargo ships, the *Argos*, had been found. Indeed, Paul, their son, and his wife Atsuko, had helped locate the sunken boat and had established that the cargo being shipped out by the Stewart-Barclays of Kincardine, was still on board, or in this case, not.

A whole fraud scheme had been uncovered which had then led to deadly consequences. That was now all in the past. The whole incident had at least brought her friend Susan Parker back to the village and, once more, into Rose and Tom's life.

Shaking her head from all her recollections Rose once again thought about Tom and his plans for this summer. He wanted her to sail with him up to Kincardine and spend the night before sailing back to Bayfield. This did not exactly excite Rose and she secretly hoped that either Tom would find someone else to crew with him, or that he would forget about the plan altogether and get too involved with playing golf or croquet as he did most summers.

Sailing was also so weather dependent. The previous summer Tom had only taken *Tranquility* out half a dozen times because the wind and weather just hadn't been in synchronicity with the days that Tom had wanted to sail.

Rose carried her cleaning materials onto the dock. She fished out the padlock key and jumped onto the boat and was about to unlock the hatch when she heard a soft thudding against the side of the boat. Rose stood up and looked over the starboard side into the space between the neighbouring boats.

There, caught between the buffers of the two boats was the body of a woman floating face down. She was wearing a pair of brown Capris and a peach-coloured blouse which now seemed to pillow out like a mushroom on each side of her. Her feet were clad in low healed peach coloured ballet pumps.

Her hair, from what Rose could see, was a sandy blond, but most of the back of her head was now missing.

Rose stifled a scream, dropped the padlock keys, and jumped onto the dock, whilst feeling for her precious phone nestled in her pocket. Tom had bought her an iPhone a couple of summers ago after she had been attacked on the beach. He had made her promise to keep it charged up and turned on. She had kept her promise and to this day she had thanked Tom for his insight.

Rose pressed the phone icon and proceeded to tap in Susan's number. She answered straight away.

"Susan, Susan, I'm down at the marina by Tom's boat and, and there's a body in the water..." Rose felt her voice thicken. How could this possibly be? Yet another murder in Bayfield?

Susan came immediately, having first called the Serious Crimes Unit, her old detachment, in London and then the local O.P.P. near Goderich. The first thing Susan did was turn the body over in the water using Tom's boat hook.

Rose watched on with sickening horror as she realized who the woman in the water was. Without doubt the victim was none other than Jan Du Preez, her friend from the safari. Although Rose averted her eyes from the body, she could not help herself being drawn to the hole at the back of her head that was now just a bloody mass of hair and bone. Rose felt bile rise in her throat and she quickly moved away and gulped it down.

The following hours were taken up with the forensics team taping off the area, then the police photographer, Peter Joyce, arrived. Susan hadn't seen him since the previous year and had forgotten how pleasant he was and how easy he was to talk to. He was a tall man with an almost gangly, loose-limbed appearance, rugged face, and a definite twinkle in his eyes.

There was, however, much to be done and once the team had arrived Susan felt that her services were no longer needed. She was after all now a retired police officer and would only get in the way of the investigation if she was to stay. She returned to her condo wishing the team well, but at the same time she felt an acute sense of loss. Being right in the thick of a murder had made Susan realize just how much she missed her job.

Not long after she got home, Susan received a telephone call from her old chief. He requested she attend an emergency meeting at the Serious Crimes Unit in London. At first, she had resented being called in as she was retired from the police force, but then curiosity had won in the end. So, it was with a sense of déjà vu that two hours later she stepped into the Chief Inspector's office and took a seat opposite him at his desk. It was funny that now that she was retired, she did not feel at all threatened by her otherwise imposing boss.

He was a big man with an air of superiority and privilege that fairly oozed out of his skin. The Chief was well respected in the force and generally treated his staff with respect. Susan smiled at him and relaxed as he shook her hand.

"Well, well, Susan, you are looking much better than last time that I saw you. Retirement obviously agrees with you."

"Yes, sir." Susan answered, "But can I ask you what it is you called me in for?"

"Straight to the point eh Susan. You haven't changed a bit, have you? But yes, I have a little proposition to make to you. We are painfully aware how short staffed we are at the moment. Your replacement, John Radcliffe, is away on a two-week vacation and we have no senior staff to head up the murder investigation in Bayfield. I know that you have firsthand experience of that village, and you are ideally placed living there right now. Would you consider being temporarily re-instated as a Detective Inspector for this case? I could second some officers from here and I am sure that the Goderich detachment might be able to spare a few officers too. We would cover your expenses as well as reinstate you at your last pay grade. What do you think?"

Susan was a little shocked. On the one hand she wasn't totally surprised as she had been the first person, other than Rose, to have been at the scene of the crime and had called in the team, but to be asked back to lead the investigation, well, that did come as a surprise. Would she be physically and mentally up to the task? Maybe it would be good for her to get back on the horse and take up the reigns again.

All these thoughts whirled through her mind as well as the picture of Rose, her dearest friend's face, absolutely devastated to find the dead woman was none other than her friend, Jan, from the African safari. Surely, if nothing else, she owed it to Rose to solve the murder at the marina.

Susan nodded her head. "Yes, I'll do it, but I want Sergeant Flowers, Sergeant Mathieson, and Constable Elliot from this division and Constable Brown from the Goderich O.P.P. They have all worked with me before and I have every faith in their abilities.

Hopefully, I'll be able to use The Lions Hall again for my meetings and that I'll have the full co-operation of Interpol, as I'm sure you know, Jan Du Preez and her husband, Andre, were on holiday from South Africa. No one has heard from Andre and there is a daughter in New York City who will need to be contacted."

As Susan spoke, the enormity of the case suddenly seemed to blow up before her eyes. All murder enquiries required tenacity, hard work, and a great deal of luck, but this case looked to be much more complicated than that with an international element. Susan felt a tingle of excitement run down her spine. Yes, this might prove to be just what she needed to get her old life back on track again.

Driving back to Bayfield, Susan went through a mental list of things that she would have to do. First and foremost, she needed to book the Lions Hall, then get her team in place. Rose and Tom Blair would have to be interviewed and the daughter contacted. One of the biggest priorities would be to track down the husband, Andre Du Preez, as he would likely hold the key to the many questions floating around this newly hatched enquiry.

THREE

After discovering the gruesome body of her friend Jan, Susan had told Rose to go home. She would interview Tom and her later that day. Rose had driven back to Bayfield Terrace in a daze. It all seemed surreal. What was her friend doing by their boat? How did Jan even know about *Tranquility*?

Then it hit Rose like a rock as she remembered clearly that day when they had driven out in the Land Rover to Lake Nyasa to see the pink flamingos. From a distance the lake had looked as if it was rose coloured when in fact it was just filled with thousands upon thousands of pink flamingos. She remembered laughing and saying to Jan, "Just imagine trying to sail a boat on that lake," and Jan had innocently asked Rose if they owned a boat and the conversation had taken a different turn with Andre and Tom talking about various types of boats that they had owned. Andre, it transpired was a keen sailor. Back in Windhoek they owned a 30-foot C&C. Tom had described his boat and talked about all sorts of technical terms which soon had Jan and Rose switched off the topic of boats. They had, however, stopped to watch a herd of elephants cross the dirt track they had been driving on and the subject of sailing had ended altogether.

Rose pulled into their driveway and glanced at her watch. Tom should have been back from golf by now, although if he had stayed on for a drink with Doug he could be much later.

She opened the front door, kicked off her shoes and collapsed on to the sofa. Suddenly the enormity of what she had witnessed overwhelmed Rose and she started to cry. Ben and Puff both padded over and licked her feet, silently willing their beloved mistress to be alright. Rose wiped her tears away with the back of her hand and took a deep breath as she patted the dogs.

"Oh, Ben and Puff, what shall I do?"

With these words out of her mouth Rose stood up and paced the floor. If Jan was dead, where was her husband Andre? What about their daughter in New York? And finally Rose thought, why, oh why, would anyone want to kill her friend Jan?

Tom arrived home shortly after Rose had found Andre and Jan's address and telephone number which she had jotted down in her journal. The same journal that she had kept while on the safari. As soon as Tom walked in Rose ran to him teary eyed and said, "Tom, Tom, Jan Du Preez is dead. Oh Tom, I found her floating face down by the side of our boat, the whole back of her head was blown off." It had all come out in a garbled flow and Tom had to slow Rose down.

"Now, love, tell me again. Did you actually say that Jan Du Preez, from the safari, was found dead here in Bayfield? That sounds so improbable. Surely you've got it wrong? It just can't be Jan Du Preez. What on earth would she be doing here in Bayfield a thousand miles away from South Africa?"

"But Tom, it definitely was Jan and yes, they were coming to visit us. Look, look at this postcard." Rose showed Tom the card sent from New York. "Look at the post date, ten days ago. They obviously rented a car and had driven up here. But where is Andre?"

Tom shook his head.

"Well, one thing is for certain, he can't be far away. My bet is that he's holed up in some motel and probably doesn't even know that his wife is dead."

"Oh Tom," Rose said looking distraught. "He'll have to be found. Oh, what about their daughter? Oh, it's just too awful for words." With that Rose began to cry again. Tom put his arms around his wife and kissed her cheeks. Ben and Puff leaned against his legs and whined softly. Rose looked at the two dogs.

"Tom, you went off to play golf this morning and left the dogs outside. They were quite distraught when I came back from Susan's. Didn't you see my note?"

Tom looked at his wife strangely.

"I did let them in my love. They were barking like crazy. How could I not hear them?"

"Well, Tom, either you're cracking up or something's not right here. When I came back from Susan's they were both shut in the garden. I let them in. What's going on here?"

Tom went quiet and then he took out his phone.

"I'm calling the police, Rose. I don't like this one single bit."

Susan had managed to secure the Lions Hall for the investigation and had been told that Sergeant Mathieson, Contables Elliot and Brown, and Sergeant Flowers were all on board. She needed, however, to interview Rose and Tom, the only two people who could shed any light on the dead woman and hopefully give the team some material to work with.

The pathologist had said that he would send his preliminary report to her by the morning and forensics were still working on the boat, dusting it for fingerprints and dredging the water for the murder weapon. It looked like a single bullet to the back of the head had killed Jan, although the time of death, the caliber of bullet, and how long she had been in the water, would all be determined by the forensic team. The whole area had been cordoned off with yellow tape.

Fortunately, it was still quiet in the village and the marina was devoid of people. The summer season had barely begun, yet in a few days, during Victoria Day weekend, everything would burst into life. All the more reason to strike while the iron was hot and sew up the crime scene before the tourists arrived.

Susan had checked to see if anyone had booked into the Cottage Colony and according to the records, nobody had. As she walked past number five, she couldn't help but recall the time spent with Jim Reynolds. Her affair with him had lasted one year and to her eternal embarrassment, had ended when she had discovered that he was involved with murder and extortion. It was Jim Reynolds who had shot and killed her fiancé, Henri Le Bruin at Centralia Airport whilst trying to leave the country with his two sons.

Susan shook her head to rid the sadness that had been her shadow for so long. Instead of dwelling on the past she smiled at the thought of meeting up with Peter Joyce, the photographer. He had been with the forensics team earlier in the day and had been totally surprised to see Susan. Peter was a freelance photographer often seconded to the police when needed. He had first met Susan the previous year when they had struck up an easy friendship.

There had been an attraction from the onset of their meeting but, at the time, Susan had been engaged to Henri. Seeing him again one year later had stirred up the old feelings which must have been reciprocated because Peter had sidled up to her just before leaving and had invited her out to dinner the upcoming Saturday. That was in three days' time but right now, Susan thought, a visit to Tom and Rose was called for and with that she jumped into her car and drove to Bayfield Terrace.

Whenever Susan drove over to visit her friends, she always felt a twinge of envy as it appeared that Rose and Tom seemed to have it all. A lovely home, a solid marriage and three delightful children. If she hadn't liked them so much, Susan would not have stayed so connected, but Rose had been kindness itself over the years and an angel this past year.

She had reached the top of Short Hill and was about to turn right onto the terrace when she saw what looked like a black bird, a large one at that, flying above Rose and Tom's house. It could have been a bird of prey or maybe a gull, but whatever it was it appeared to be circling their home. Susan stopped looking just in time to pull into their driveway and soon all thoughts of the bird were pushed away as Tom opened the door.

"Wow, that was quick. I've just put the phone down. Impressive."

Susan looked quizzically at Tom.

"Tom, what on earth are you on about? I've just popped over to ask you and Rose a few questions about Jan Du Preez."

Tom coughed and explained how he had just phoned the O.P.P. and told Susan about the dogs being shut out of the house."

"Have you checked the house to see if anything has been taken?" Susan asked as she wrote down the details. "It strikes me that whoever broke into your house must have been looking for something specific otherwise your place would have been ransacked."

Tom and Rose had indeed made a thorough search of their home and could not find anything missing or even out of place.

"So, I assume that the house was left unlocked as I could see no signs of forced entry? You know that I've warned you before about leaving your house unlocked. There are predators out there and it could invalidate your insurance policy too. I'm sure that I've told you both this before?"

Both Tom and Rose were guilty of never locking up their house or cars except at nighttime. They had been told off before and now stood humbled before Susan who smiled and patted Rose on her shoulder before saying. "Don't look so glum. Now could you both tell me all that you know about Jan du Preez?"

FOUR

Susan looked around the room where her team were all gathered. The Lions Hall almost felt like a second home to her now having used it three times already for previous cases.

A white board and an incident board had been set up by the chalk board at the head of the room. The Lions Hall had once been the Bayfield Village School consisting of just two large classrooms. The school had been closed in the 1970s when the new school to serve the hamlets of Varna and Brucefield, Stanley Township, and the Village of Bayfield had been built just outside of Brucefield on Highway 8. After serving as the village municipal offices up until the amalgamation into the Municipality of Bluewater, the Lions club had taken over the operation of the building and had used it ever since for community events and for their meetings.

Mathieson had grown a beard since Susan had last seen him and Susan also discovered that he had also been promoted to Sergeant. She had in fact not recognized him when he first entered the room. Taking him to one side, she congratulated him on his promotion. Constable Elliot also looked different, and Susan couldn't quite put a finger on why, but he certainly appeared more confident. Constables Brown and Sergeant Flowers looked the same.

Susan stepped forward to welcome her team.

"Right, everyone, welcome back to Bayfield. We have much to discuss and very little to go on. Jan du Preez was found murdered down at the marina. Her body was discovered floating in the water by the side of Rose and Tom Blair's boat called *Tranquility*. The preliminary pathologist's report states that the cause of death was from a single 9mm 38 caliber bullet fired at close range. As there was no blood on the boat, we can assume that the massive impact of the bullet hitting her head caused the victim to fall into the water. We are waiting to hear if she was dead before hitting the water or not. A postmortem is being conducted as we speak.

"Jan Du Preez and her husband, Andre, according to Rose Blair, were in Bayfield to visit them although neither of them had shown up at their house. They had flown to New York from Johannesburg where they were visiting their daughter Lora Du Preez. Rose received a postcard from the couple saying that they were going to rent a car and drive to Bayfield to visit them.

"Now, one of our first tasks is to track down the rented car and hopefully that might lead us to Andre. Sergeant Mathieson, I would like you to check with the Canadian Border Securities along all the main entry points to Canada. I would imagine that they would have entered Canada via Buffalo but check with Montreal and all the other border entry points from New York State. There will be a record of their date of entry and more importantly, their hire car license plate number. Check all CCTV footage. It is imperative that we track down the hire car as that could lead us to Andre Du Preez.

"Constable's Brown and Elliot check out the motels and B&B's

in this area and then show this photograph that I got from Rose Blair and ask around the village. Someone must have seen them.

"On a separate note, which may or may not be related to this case, Tom and Rose Blair have had their house broken into and, although nothing appears to have been taken, it all seems a bit of a coincidence that this should happen at the same time as the murder. I, as you all know, don't believe in coincidences. We need to be vigilant. Sergeant Flowers, you can organize a house-to-house check and ask anyone if they have seen anyone new in the neighbourhood."

Sergeant Mathieson cleared his throat and put up his hand to gain Susan's attention.

"Um, Ma'am, do we know anything about Andre Du Preez? In 95% of murder enquiries, as I'm sure you know," Susan bristled at the Sergeant's tone of voice, "it is the husband who is the perpetrator. What sort of relationship did he have with his wife?"

"Good question, Sergeant, and, so far, we only have Rose and Tom's word on what they know about the Du Preez's and, to be quite frank, they only met them recently on an African safari and how much can anyone know about another in just ten days?

"I have contacted Interpol to see if they have anything on the Du Preez's and I have also sent out a request to the Windhoek Constabulary in Namibia to see if they can rustle up some background information on Andre Du Preez. I'm afraid it's going to be a waiting game for now.

"Okay, so let's go to it. Let's reconvene at the same time tomorrow."

The team ambled out leaving Susan to type up her report to the Chief at the London office. *What a lame report,* she thought as she concluded her statement and pressed *send.* Her mind wandered over the meeting that she had just had with her team.

What was wrong with Sergeant Mathieson? Had his promotion gone to his head? He had appeared almost aggressive in his behaviour. She would have to keep an eye out for him, as she couldn't afford to have her team compromised by one wild card.

FIVE

Rose had spent the morning baking. She had made Abby and Ella's favourite spaghetti pie and chocolate walnut cake. Maybe she could bake Jessica's much loved rhubarb custard pie if there was enough rhubarb left to be picked in the garden. She called to the dogs who had flopped down in the sunroom. It was time that they had some fresh air. *Maybe Tom could be coaxed into taking them for a walk,* Rose thought as she went into the garden. For that matter, where was Tom? She hadn't seen him all morning.

It wasn't long before Rose had an answer to her question. She heard an almighty thump and then a loud curse followed by a very dusty, dirty looking Tom.

"What on earth have you been doing, darling? You're covered in dirt."

"I've been in the garage trying to sort out the mess. Honestly, Rose, we need to get rid of some of those suitcases. We've got ten in all different shapes and sizes. When is it the town wide garage sale?"

Rose laughed, "Oh, Tom, it's this weekend and yes, we can get rid of most of the stuff in the garage, but I don't want to sit outside and sell it myself. Look, I tell you what, Lena's definitely having a garage sale and I'm sure she won't mind if I gave her some more things to sell."

Tom was about to answer when the telephone rang. Rose ran into the house to grab the phone and was thoroughly annoyed when all there was silence on the other end of the line. This was the third time Rose had encountered the 'silent' treatment. She fairly shouted down the phone, "For heaven's sake say something or stop phoning this number."

She was about to slam down the phone when a voice, a familiar voice, whispered.

"Rose, I need to speak to Tom."

"Andre, is that you? Where are you?"

"Rose, please, please get Tom to the phone."

Andre sounded desperate. Rose ran to the back of the house and shouted to Tom.

"Tom, Tom, come quickly. It's Andre on the phone."

Tom ran inside and grabbed the phone off Rose who hovered close by trying to hear what Andre had to say.

Tom listened intently, his face scrunched up with concentration. His voice sounded strained as he spoke to Andre.

"So, let me get this straight. You want to meet me tonight down on Pavilion Road? Seven o'clock? Okay, will do, but Andre, you have a lot of answering to do and this better be up front, with no tricks."

Tom put the phone down and raised his shoulders, shrugged, sighing loudly as he told Rose his plans.

"But love, don't you think that we should let Susan know?" Rose said anxiously.

"Look, Rose, I owe it to Andre to at least hear him out. If I smell a rat, then I'll phone Susan straight away and if I'm not back by 8:30 you must call her yourself."

"Oh, darling, please be careful."

The phone rang again, and Rose nearly jumped out of her skin with fright. It was Paul phoning from London. Paul had returned from Japan the previous summer to take up a position at Fanshawe College. He had left his wife, Atsuko behind on the understanding that he would return to Japan during the college vacation. Rose and Tom had expected Paul to have returned to his wife now that college was out for the summer, but, to their consternation, he had shown no sign of leaving.

"Hi, Mom. Just planning to check if it's still on for Sunday? Also, could I bring Marty with me?"

"Well, yes, but who is Marty?" Rose asked while frowning at the phone.

"Oh, well, she's, umm.... a French girl that I met. She's studying economics here at Fanshawe. You'll love her."

There was a pause before Rose could speak.

"Umm...Paul, what about Atsuko?"

Paul cleared his throat and, with a low voice said.

"Mom, Atsuko and I are finished. She's made it very clear that she doesn't want anything more to do with me. Besides, she's met another man. I don't want to talk about it."

"Oh, darling, I'm so sorry. Your father and I are very fond of Atsuko. Are you sure that your marriage is over? Shouldn't you just fly over to Japan and try to save it?"

"Mom, she doesn't want me anymore. There's no point in me wasting all that money on an air ticket when she quite emphatically has told me we're over. I just want to move on."

"Well, love, you're welcome to bring this French girl, Marty, to lunch, but my advice to you is that it's too soon to be thinking about starting up another relationship."

Rose put the phone down and turned to Tom. In an exasperated voice she said. "Oh, Tom, it looks as if Paul and Atsuko have split up. I want to knock their silly heads together and I blame Paul for leaving Atsuko alone all these months. He should never have taken that job in London. Don't they realize that you have to work at marriage and fight for it too? Oh, it makes me feel so sad."

Tom put his arms around her shoulders and pulled her against his chest. He held her tightly and gently kissed the top of her head.

"Don't worry my love, they'll find their way. If it's meant to be, it's meant to be. As much as we love Atsuko, Paul has to make his own decisions. Now I'm going to drive all this junk from the garage over to Lena's and then I'll come back and make us a nice gin and tonic. We can relax on the patio before supper. In fact, why don't I just throw some salmon on the barbeque, and we can have that with a tossed salad?"

Rose smiled at her husband. She did love him so and was about to give Tom a kiss when the phone rang again.

Tom answered. "Oh, hi Peggy. Yes, she's right here, just one minute while I get her."

Tom turned and called to Rose who was back in the kitchen.

"Darling, phone's for you. It's Peggy."

Peggy was the Chair of the Town Hall Committee which Rose had joined the previous year. There had been a ghastly murder when the leader of a band, The Berries, had been found dead in the 'jail' of the Town Hall.

It had been Peggy who had discovered Joe Berry covered in blood, a knife protruding from his neck. What had made matters worse was the knife had been one of a new set Rose had purchased from a kitchen shop in Goderich. Rose and Tom had been helping the evening of the concert and it was Rose who had tried to calm down the almost hysterical Peggy.

Now, a year later, Rose felt like she had sat on the Town hall

Committee forever. It was a very busy, hard-working group and they seemed to be forever fundraising to keep the old building alive.

Rose picked up the phone and said,

"Hi, Peggy, how can I help you?"

Peggy, who was the most efficient and organized person Rose had ever known replied. "Rose, we have a Town Hall Committee meeting coming up and I can't make it. It took me ages to find a date when everyone could attend and so I am loathed to change it now. I wonder if you could chair the meeting in my absence."

Rose had never chaired anything before and was reluctant to do so. She did, however, feel sorry for Peggy. The last few meetings had been really spotty with few board members in attendance. The big trouble was that at least half the members were 'snow-birds' who disappeared down south for the winter and who only started to return in dribs and drabs after Easter.

"But Peggy, I don't think I could chair a meeting. I'd be useless at it."

"Now, Rose, that's ridiculous. You were once a teacher, just put on your teacher voice. Look, I've got everything ready, you just have to go through last month's minutes, get all the approvals, which won't be at all difficult as we didn't even have a quorum. The biggest item on the agenda is, Sunset on Summer. I need to get volunteers signed up for the event."

Rose interrupted Peggy.

"Peggy, Sunset on Summer isn't until Labour Day weekend which is still three months away."

'Rose, we have to start planning now. I've already booked the chicken people. We have to book the music, start the publicity, work out who will make the salads, get the corn, and so it goes on. There is so much to be organized and I've itemized everything in my notes here for you."

Rose still thought that it was somewhat advanced planning, but she also knew that Peggy was right. Once summer got going it would just whiz by in a flash.

"Alright, Peggy, I'll do it. Can you drop off the minutes and agenda before the meeting?"

Peggy replied crisply,

"But I've already sent it all out to the Board Members by email. Did you not get it?"

Rose had not checked her emails for a few days and she suddenly felt rather guilty. Some of her friends were on their computers for hours each day, and even had time to check out their Facebook pages, but somehow Rose never seemed to have the time to spare.

Tom would be the one to see photographs posted from Jessica or Anne on Facebook and he would draw Rose's attention to other interesting posts. She seemed far busier in retirement than before when she was teaching. It was all the committees that she had got sucked into that had done it, Rose thought, although she wouldn't change any of it because she loved her life in the village of Bayfield.

Susan glanced once again at the report sent from the Windhoek constabulary. She had asked them to verify the existence of Jan and Andre Du Preez and for any further information known about the couple. What they sent read like some executive's biography. Jan and Andre had certainly not been ordinary people. Both their careers had records of achievement far above the norm. If success was to be measured by the incomes that they both earned, which in their cases were well above six figures, they were on par with the rich and the famous. Andre and Jan worked for De Beer Diamonds and were both top executives.

Susan looked down at her finger where her engagement ring sparkled with sapphires and diamonds. Her eyes welled up with tears as she recalled Henri, her late fiancé, her handsome French man from Montreal, proposing to her.

Diamonds were not forever, Susan thought as she slipped the beautiful ring off her finger and held it up against her heart. Maybe it was time to put the ring away and move on with her life.

As for Andre and Jan, they had been with De Beers for thirty years and as such had worked their way up the ladder of success. There appeared to be nothing suspicious about their employment. They had nothing but glowing reports throughout the course of both their careers.

Back on Bayfield Terrace, Tom kissed Rose goodbye and got into his sports car, an Audi TT. He had driven it from the garage where it had been stored for the winter and, as soon as the snow was off the ground, Tom had taken the car out for a spin. He had in a surprising move, bought the sleek sports car just two years previously and Rose had claimed it was part of his male menopause. She did, however, secretly admire the beautiful car, his 'man toy.'

Tom had put the roof down as it was a fine summers evening. The sky was a thrush egg blue with fluffy white clouds dotted here and there. Driving along Bayfield Terrace to Short Hill and then onto the highway, Tom smiled to himself. Life was good. He just loved the village of Bayfield and his life with Rose. He was, however, feeling decidedly uncertain about his meeting with Andre Du Preez. Without doubt he had enjoyed the man's company when they were on the safari in Kenya and Tom had always prided himself on being a good judge of character, but everyone knew that the husband was more often than not the murderer when it came to a crime of passion. However, Andre had appeared to be the genuine loving husband to a lovely wife. At the thought of Jan, Tom wondered if Andre even knew that his wife was dead, assuming that he was in fact innocent of the crime. *Oh, my God, I might have to break the news to him,* he thought.

Driving past Sugar Bush Road, Tom wondered how his golfing buddy, Ian was after his triple bypass heart surgery. Ian had been playing golf when he had collapsed suddenly, and if it hadn't had been for the speedy actions of the paramedic who had arrived quickly after the 911 call, he would never have survived. *You just never knew when life was going to throw you a curve ball,* Tom thought as he turned onto Pavilion Road.

He could see what looked like a white Toyota Camry in the car park by the Pavilion at the end of the road. As Tom pulled in alongside the car, he realized that someone was slumped over the steering wheel. Jumping out of the car with a sinking feeling in the pit of his belly, Tom ran over to the Camry and pulled open the driver's door. Andre's head was down, but he was still sitting in the driver's seat. Most of the back of his head had been blown off leaving a grizzly mess of pulped brain, hair, and presumably mashed bone.

Tom felt his stomach heave. He looked around him and all was peaceful outside with no sign of another living soul in sight. He took a second closer look at Andre and noticed straight away a small piece of paper tucked into the top pocket of his bloodied shirt. Without stopping to think, Tom leant into the car and pulled out the scrap of paper. He stared at the row of numbers scrawled across with the single word 'TAS' underneath. Tom stuffed the paper into his pocket as he pulled out his cell phone. He first called 911 and gave all the details to the Dispatch Officer. Then he tapped in Susan Parker's number and went back to his car to wait.

Rose looked at her watch for the tenth time. Tom should have been back ages ago as it was already 9:30 and beginning to get dark. All evening Rose had felt an uneasy sense of disquiet. Puff and Ben obviously felt it too as they had been incredibly restless, wanting to go out and in all evening, to the point that Rose had gone out with them and walked around the garden to see if maybe a racoon or skunk had wandered in and were causing the dogs to be agitated. Looking up at the sky she noticed the black crow flying above. Funny, she thought, they never had crows soaring above their house before. Finally at ten o'clock Tom appeared looking positively exhausted.

"Where have you been, love?" Rose exclaimed as she kissed him on his cheek, "I've been so worried about you."

Tom slumped himself into one of the armchairs. Running his hand through his hair he sighed.

"Oh, Rose, I found Andre dead in his car. It was terrible. I had to wait for the police and then I was questioned forever and, I have to say, admonished for not telling them about my meeting with Andre. Susan really laid into me telling me that we are to back off and leave the police to do their jobs."

Rose poured Tom out a beer and brought it over to him. Puff and Ben lay down at his feet, instantly calming down now that their master had returned.

"They've been so restless, love. We were all on edge waiting for you. How dreadful though, both Andre and Jan dead. Tom, what on earth is going on?"

"I don't know, Rose, but somehow we've got ourselves involved."

Rose looked as if she was about to cry again, "Tom, their poor daughter, Lora, is now an orphan. I must contact her. I wonder if Susan would be able to give me her contact details. All I know is that she lives in New York somewhere."

"I'd leave it be for a few days, love. Your friend was pretty angry with me this evening. She really doesn't want us getting involved."

"Well," Rose retorted, "Jan and Andre were our friends and, of course we would want to send our condolences to their daughter. I'll speak to Susan tomorrow. I'm going to bed now. I need to think. Something big is happening and I feel greatly disturbed. Goodnight, Tom."

Tom sat in the dark for another ten minutes trying to process what was going on. Somehow Rose and he had got tied up in murder and intrigue all because of befriending a couple of nice people thousands of miles away from home while on a safari in Africa. *Bizarre*, Tom thought as he finished off his beer and rose to go to bed. One thing was for certain, though, Tom thought, the whole business had upset Rose deeply, and that wouldn't do.

SIX

S usan got up early and, lacing up her shoes, she stepped out into the fresh dew-soaked morning. She missed the indoor swimming pool of what used to be the Bayfield Village Inn and that was now called 'The Ashwood Inn.'

The next best thing to swimming however, was running, and Susan needed the adrenalin rush to help clear her head. Running down Jowett's Grove, she turned right and ran on past the Cottage Colony down to the marina. She stopped there and looked out towards the lake. The water was calm and gentle with a light, fluffy morning mist just hovering over the surface.

Susan turned her gaze over towards the boats moored beneath her. There was one new looking boat, forty foot long, sleek and black with a tall antenna winding itself out of the cockpit onto a small satellite dish attached to the roof. It was a power boat, an expensive one at that.

I wonder who that expensive boat belongs to? Susan thought while turning her head to look back towards the Cottage Colony.

She could see the yellow police tape surrounding the docks gently flapping in the breeze. No one would even begin to guess that such a gruesome murder had just taken place there in such an idyllic setting. Susan looked at her watch, turned and sprinted all the way that she had come, back up the hill to her condo. She would just about have enough time to take a shower and be at the Lions Hall in time for their morning's debriefing.

Rose and Tom woke up after a restless night's sleep. Rose had been dreaming about Andre and Jan on safari. In her dream Jan was pointing towards a clump of acacia trees as Andre beckoned to Tom and her to come over. Just as they had almost reached the trees a flash of yellow streaked past. Jan screamed as the fearsome leopard pounced upon her.

Rose woke up with a jolt before she knew what the outcome was of the attack. Tom, on the other hand, had been reliving in full technicolour, the discovery of Andre shot dead in his car. His dream was like watching a movie set in an endless loop. Tom opened his eyes and sat bolt upright. He had just remembered something.

Jumping out of bed, he ran over to the chair where he had dumped all his clothes the night before. Putting his hand into his shirt pocket he pulled out the slip of paper he had found in Andre's pocket. Rose looked up at Tom and said, "What on earth are you doing Tom?"

Tom held up the piece of paper and read out the single word written above the row of numbers. "TAS."

"That sounds like some sort of code," Rose said as she stared at the piece of paper now lying on the bedside table beside her.

"I reckon that this word is Afrikaans or Dutch. Why don't you use Google to translate it and see what it says, Tom?"

Tom pulled out his smartphone and within minutes he had the translation.

"You were right, love. Tas means suitcase in Afrikaans. So... that still doesn't help us much."

Rose thought a minute. "Maybe the numbers are some kind of code. Oh, I don't know. Do you think that we should tell Susan?"

At the mention of Susan, Tom once more felt chastened. She had well and truly snapped at him at Pavillion Road, and he did not want to face her again so soon after his slap on the wrists.

"No, let's just give it a bit of thought first. Those numbers must mean something."

Rose was prevented from saying anything further by the telephone ringing. It was Lena asking her if she still wanted to bring things around for the garage sale.

With all the comings and goings of the previous twenty-four hours they had both completely forgotten about the pile of sorted items that Tom had thrown out of the garage. Rose told Lena that one of them would drop everything off later that day.

"Thanks so much, Lena. You're a star." Rose said as she put the phone down and got out of bed.

"Right, breakfast calls, Tom, and then we must load all of the garage sale items into the car ready to take around to Lena's. While you do that, I'll take the dogs for a walk."

The two of them finished getting up and soon Rose had the coffee put on and eggs on the go. A new day had dawned along with a new problem to solve. What did those numbers mean?

SEVEN

T he team were all assembled and keen to get started. Susan smiled and looked at her watch. It was only 7:45 yet everyone was bright eyed and bushy tailed and obviously raring to go. Running had cleared her head and she, too, was pumped up.

"Good morning everyone, let's hear your reports before we move on to the latest murder, that of Andre Du Preez, Jan Du Preez's husband. Firstly, Sergeant Mathieson, anything to report on the car rental and border security?"

Sergeant Mathieson stood up clutching a pile of computer print offs.

"Yes, well, Jan and Andre Du Preez entered Canada at the Buffalo border crossing. The CCTV footage clearly shows them sitting in a white Toyota Camry at 9:00 a.m. on May 20th, with New York license plates. I managed to track down the car rental to Hertz, New York City, and they confirmed that Jan and Andre Du Preez from Windhoek, Namibia, rented the vehicle for a two-week period starting May 19th and finishing June 2nd. They paid the extra $50 to leave the car at the Hertz deposit site by Pearson

Airport in Toronto, when they were due to fly back to Namibia. That is all I have to report, Ma'am."

"Thank you, Sergeant," Susan said, "Constable Brown, any luck with the motels?"

Constable Brown looked down at his notes and then stood up to speak.

"Yes, Ma'am. We found the Du Preez's registered at the Hampton Inn just across the border in Niagara. That was on May 19th. Rose Blair found the body of Jan Du Preez on May 20th. We found no further motel bookings in this area registered in their names."

Constable Brown sat down.

"Thank you, Constable. Has anyone got anything further to add?"

"Yes, Ma'am," Constable Elliot said as he stood up. "A man matching Andre Du Preez's description was seen having lunch at the Hessenland Inn yesterday. He stayed for a long time, and, according to the waitress whom I spoke with," the Constable referred to his notes, "Her name is Stella Bryant. Stella says that Andre appeared restless and extremely agitated. At one point he left the dining room and she watched him pull out his cell phone and speak to someone. She said that he looked furtive, kept looking around the room as if he was afraid of someone or something. He finally left at about 3:30 p.m. That's all I have to report, Ma'am."

"Thank you, Constable. Well team, it appears that our prime suspect in the murder of Jan Du Preez is now himself dead, thus eliminating him from our enquiry."

Sergeant Mathieson cleared his throat and then stood up quickly saying, "But excuse me, Andre could still have murdered his wife and then been eliminated himself. It's not likely, but we cannot categorically rule him out."

Susan felt irritated by Sergeant Mathieson's aggressive stance.

He was right, of course and she knew it, but it was his attitude that had irked her more than anything else.

"Yes, you are correct, Sergeant, and we will have to wait for the forensic report before we jump to any conclusions. But, on face value, it does look as though it was the same gun used to kill both Andre and Jan. Since this clearly was no suicide then it definitely points to a third party. Forensics are working on the tire tracks found next to the victim's car. Similar car tracks were found at The Cottage Colony.

"But what I want to know is where Andre was hiding these past few days since his wife's death. If the Du Preez were last seen together at the Hampton Inn outside of Niagara, then that narrows the date to May 20th when they checked out of the hotel. Later that day at 2:30 p.m., to be precise, the body of Jan Du Preez was found by Rose Blair in the marina."

Susan paused and looked down at her notes before continuing,

"Andre, however, was not found until yesterday, two days later. Where was he, and what was he doing these past few days? Do we even have any idea who might have been following Andre and Jan? Up until now we have been too focused on finding Andre. We need to double back to the beginning and really focus on the marina. Constable Elliot, go and question everyone you can at the marina, the docks, and conduct a house-to-house interview to the residents of Hidden Valley and Harbour Lights. Someone must have seen something somewhere.

"Sergeant Mathieson, I want you to do the same down Pavillion and Ravine Roads and then come back to the village and ask the shopkeepers if they have noticed any strange activities. Someone will have seen something out of the ordinary, I'm sure. Go and talk to the couple who own the coffee shop, Shop Bike, as they seem to be at the hub of the village in terms of information.

We need results. It is already three days since the first murder, and time is ticking by."

Susan turned and picked up a folder sitting on her desk.

"What I do have is a detailed report on the Du Preez's from the Windhoek police. Andre was CEO of the De Beers IT department. He had been employed by them for over 30 years and was largely responsible for programming all the high-level security. Jan worked in the accounts department. Both earned six figure salaries, and both were senior executives. Pictures of their house in Windhoek show a degree of high living only associated with the really well-to-do." Susan pinned up a photograph of an ultra-modern two-story white structure complete with an infinity pool which looked as if it had come straight out of the centre pages of a *Home and Garden* magazine.

Susan continued. "Their daughter, Lora Du Preez, works for the UN in New York as a systems analyst. She is thirty-four, single, and very much a career girl. We have contacted her, and she will be flying out tomorrow. I might get a better picture of her parents after interviewing her, we'll have to see. Hopefully forensics will have their report done by tomorrow. I have a meeting with the Chief, and I know that he will want to hear that we have made some progress with this case. Let's try to crack open this murder. Just go to it and bring me back some results."

The men shuffled out of the Lions Hall; their otherwise sunny disposition now clouded over. Susan looked again at the text message from her boss.

"Need to see you immediately. Be at my office at 2:00 p.m. this afternoon."

What could be so urgent, Susan thought as she put away her computer and stood up ready to go.

Rose clipped Puff and Ben's leashes on and, grabbing some plastic bags, she opened the front door ready to take the dogs for a walk. She was about to set off down the driveway when she stopped, went back to the front door, and locked it. Normally Tom and she never locked the house up, but Susan had been so annoyed with them over their casual attitude towards security and with the recent murders, it all added to Rose's sense of disquiet. She would, from now on, lock the front door at least.

It was a beautiful Friday morning. Rose set off towards Louisa Street and headed in the direction of Clan Gregor Square. They would be setting up for the Farmers Market which ran throughout the summer and was open every week on a Friday from 2:00 p.m. until 7:00 p.m. It was a delightful little market, selling locally grown produce and meats.

The cheese stand selling goat and sheep's cheese was Rose's favourite and the organically grown vegetables, too. She, however, wasn't sure if the market would be open that day or whether the first market of the season started the following week after Victoria Day weekend. She would pop into the library and speak to Angela, the librarian, who was a fountain of all knowledge regarding events happening in the village.

Walking down Louisa Street, Rose passed the spot where the Gemeinhardt family had an apple orchard over a hundred years ago. They were renowned for their furniture making, but what village folklore proclaimed, was the stories of drunken pigs swaying around the place having being fed the swill from alcoholic schnapps being made on the farm. *Drunken pigs in Bayfield, what a laugh*, Rose thought.

She turned her head, looked back the way she had just come and noticed once again the black crow that she could see hovering over their house. Well, she assumed that it was the same crow, although looking at it again from that angle she began to wonder. Was it a crow, as after all it did appear to be flying around in exactly the same spot as before? Did crows return to the same spot?

She did not know the answers, but there was definitely something strange about the bird-like object hovering over their house.

Ben barked and then his whole body convulsed into a joyous wagging of his tail. Puff just stood his ground and watched as Lena approached from across the park.

"Lena, how great to see you. Did Tom catch you in? He was going to drop off a whole load of stuff for the garage sale. By the way, do you need me to help you at all? I could come for an hour or two if you want."

Lena volunteered at the Historical Society Archives and did quite amazing things with her graphic arts background. She was a bit younger than Rose and much slimmer with a pretty, round face and long, gingery hair which she mostly wore back in a ponytail.

She smiled affectionately at her friend, Rose, who looked a little pink cheeked and disheveled, which was unusual as she normally was quite well turned out.

"Yes, Tom has just left. That was quite the collection of suitcases, are you sure that you want to get rid of them all? Some look in good condition, I always reckon that if they have wheels and a handle then they're worth keeping, just for the convenience. How we managed in the old days with lugging those handheld cases around is beyond me."

Lena had mentioned the word suitcases several times. Suddenly Rose's eyes lit up. Hadn't Andre Du Preez written the Afrikaans word for 'suitcase' on the slip of paper carrying all those numbers tucked into his pocket? *Could it be as simple as that*, Rose thought.

"Lena, if you don't mind, can I come over to your place and have another look at those suitcases that Tom rather hastily threw out?"

"Sure, Rose, I'm just on my way to the Heritage Centre, but I'll be back home after lunch. Why don't you swing by for a cup of tea, and I'll fish out those cases for you to sort through. Say about two o'clock?"

"Great," Rose said. "Now, these dogs are really tugging at their leashes, I'll have to get going. See you later, Lena."

Rose continued on her way. She saw Susan Parker's car parked outside the Lion's Hall and two other O.P.P. vehicles. *I wonder how the investigations are going,* she thought as she walked down Jane Street towards the lake.

It was one of those idyllic days when the sky was completely devoid of clouds like a picture painted blue. There was a small breeze, but a southerly wind which blew warm air into Rose's face. She reached Tuyl Street and proceeded to walk towards Pioneer Park. When she got there, Rose stood on top of the stairs going down to the beach looking out at the mighty Lake Huron before her.

The sight of the lake in all its majesty always made Rose feel humble. Nature was so powerful. It had taken the lives of so many over the centuries and would continue to do so until the end of time. *If only man would respect the water more,* Rose thought as she unleashed the dogs and headed down the steps to the beach which was empty with not a single person in sight.

Soon that would change with the holiday weekend upon them. Tourists would start to trickle in, and the cottages would be filled up again as the population of the village tripled in size. The shop keepers and restauranteurs would breathe a sigh of relief as their busy season started, that would only last a mere four months. This was the time of the year Rose liked the most when everything came to life again after the sleepy, cocoon like winter. Come July and August, the village would be crazy busy, but for the next month life would just gradually pick up momentum.

Puff and Ben made a beeline for the water. They both loved swimming, although Puff would only go in if Rose threw a stick. After twenty minutes of throwing sticks Rose called both wet dogs over and leashed them, proceeding to walk along the beach towards the pier. There were no cars in the parking lot and only a few boats moored up at the public marina docks. Rose decided to walk the dogs to the Mara Street walkway and then back up to Bayfield Terrace.

She absolutely adored the tunnel of trees and ivy-covered path, even though the walk itself was pretty steep.

Arriving at the top she gulped in some deep breaths. *I should probably go back to my fitness classes,* Rose thought as she collected her breath and started walking towards their house. She was almost home when Rose spotted a large, black van with tinted windows parked just around the corner. *Strange,* she thought, she hadn't seen the van before. It looked suspiciously sinister with its black tinted glass and body, maybe it was a minister's car or some other government official's vehicle.

Puff and Ben tugged hard at their leashes as they reached their driveway. *Home sweet home,* Rose thought as she unlocked the front door and stepped inside to the coolness of the lobby. Time for a cup of tea.

EIGHT

S usan sat in front of her boss, the Chief Superintendent, in stunned silence. Surely she had not heard him correctly? Shut down the murder enquiry? Not over my dead body, Susan thought and then hoped that her thoughts were not too transparent.

She eventually found her tongue and rather hoarsely said, "Um. So, you say that CSIS have taken over the investigation? What local knowledge do they have, may I ask, sir? I understand the sensitive nature of dealing with Interpol. Good God, you of all people, sir, know that I've spent years dealing with Interpol in our search for Jim Reynolds. Look, Chief, we have a good track record, I cannot let my team down now not when we're just beginning to crack open the case. Can't we just continue doing our jobs and leave CSIS to do theirs?"

The Chief sat there in silence, brooding like a dark horse. Susan could see that he was weighing everything up. He had always been a fair man and she could see how this would be a big conflict for him. Finally, after an eternal wait, he spoke to Susan.

"Susan, even I don't have the details of what CSIS is investigating, but it must be of great significance; I'm thinking it has to be on a global scale for them to even be involved. If I allow you to continue the investigation it would be totally under the understanding that you report all your findings directly to me, and I mean, all your findings.

I will contact CSIS personally. You have to continue the enquiry knowing that you will be watched. I believe that CSIS even has a drone positioned over the Blair's house. I have to tell you that Rose and Tom right now are their prime suspects."

Susan laughed out loud.

"With all due respect, sir, that is ridiculous. Rose and Tom Blair are good people. Andre and Jan Du Preez, the couple who were murdered, were friends of theirs and nothing more. They would never, ever, be involved with anything illegal. I know them well enough to say that with absolute certainty. I mean, for heaven's sake, Rose has helped me on several occasions in solving some awful murders. No, I stand by my convictions that Rose and Tom are not involved, other than by association, with whatever CSIS is investigating."

The Chief looked thoughtful and then slowly spoke, "Well, Susan, I believe you, but it could be that they have unknowingly become pawns in a very dangerous game. Be careful. From the little that I am privy to knowing, CSIS is dealing with something far bigger than just vengeful murder. Now, have I made it perfectly clear how important it is that you report directly to me, and only me. Walls have ears and for all I know CSIS might have already infiltrated our Headquarters. Also, watch your own team. Trust no one, do you understand?"

Susan could see that the Chief was in dead earnest. She had never known him to be so melodramatic as he was normally such a pragmatist. The case must be very important and truly of international importance. She would have to tread very carefully indeed.

With her meeting concluded Susan's thoughts changed to another matter. She was going on a date the next day and she didn't have anything to wear. She would swing by the mall to try to find an outfit suitable for a first date. Thinking of Peter Joyce, the police photographer, put a smile back on her face. She was more than ready now to think about another relationship. Susan had loved Henri passionately and her memories of him would never die, but life had to go on and, if she was totally honest, she was horribly lonely. She needed someone in her life.

Tom got back just in time for lunch. He had gone off early in the morning to play a game of golf with Doug. They had driven down the lake past St. Joseph's to the Bayview golf course, but halfway through the game, Doug had felt sick and had left rather abruptly at the 12th hole.

Normally a game would have lasted most of the day by the time they had been to the club house and had a round of drinks, so Rose was quite surprised to see him walk in at noon. She had, fortunately, just baked a quiche and was just preparing a salad when Puff and Ben greeted Tom effusively, tails wagging and their faces smiling. Tom kissed Rose on her cheek and went to lay the table for lunch. While they were eating Rose told Tom her revelation about the suitcases.

"Tom, we need to search through those cases that Lena has for the garage sale. Didn't you get rid of that red one? You know my small carry on which had a broken wheel. Remember, I took that with me to South Africa. I bet you that Andre and Jan have put something in that case."

Tom thought for a minute. "You know love, you could be right. We'll both go around to Lena's and see what we can find."

They were halfway through their lunch when Rose remembered the black crow-like object.

"Tom, have you noticed something strange hovering over our house? It looks like a crow, but it doesn't seem to move. Can you go outside and have a look?"

Rose could see by the incredulous look on Tom's face that he wasn't taking her seriously. *He doesn't believe me,* Rose thought as she put away the remains of the quiche and tidied up the dining room table.

Ten minutes later Tom returned with a puzzled look on his face.

"You know something, love, that crow is as much a bird as my big toe. You know what I think it is, it's a drone and I also know something else. I walked Ben and Puff around the corner and there was a black van with tinted windows parked in front of Simon and Drew's house. I reckon it's a surveillance job. That crow has been watching us."

"My gosh, Tom, that's scary. Why would anyone want to watch us? I'm going to call Susan. That makes me feel really weird knowing that every move we make has been recorded by someone."

"Don't worry, love. I'm sure that there's a reason and a simple explanation for it all."

But Rose couldn't stop herself worrying. There were too many unexplained happenings going on in Bayfield and she did not like it one single bit.

Susan got back to Bayfield later that afternoon. She had been unsuccessful in getting a new outfit to wear for her date with Peter Joyce as her heart had not been into shopping.

The meeting with the Chief had thoroughly disturbed her and, for the first time in her long career, Susan was unsure of herself. How could she continue the investigation while tiptoeing around the big elephant in the room, CSIS?

Should she inform her team or keep it to herself? And, what if someone on her team was working as a mole for CSIS? All those thoughts and more had whirled around her head and left her feeling numb and thoroughly exhausted. It was time to quietly review all the notes and move forward with a plan. Her thoughts, however, were interrupted by her cell phone ringing. It was Tom Blair, a very agitated Tom, asking if she could come around as they had something to show her. Susan grabbed her notebook and jumped into her car. She could have walked the short distance from Harbour Court to Bayfield Terrace but had decided to go on to the Lions Hall after her meeting with Tom and Rose.

Tom was standing in their driveway waiting for Susan, a worried look furrowed across his rugged face. The old feeling of attraction stirred within Susan as she looked at her best friend's husband. She had once foolishly kissed him, and the memory of that delicious kiss still managed to evoke strong sensual chemistry within her.

Tom had been perfectly chivalrous afterwards and had made it quite plain that he was happily married to Rose, but still, she couldn't help herself as every time she was close to him the flame ignited between them once more like some unquenchable fire. She pulled into the driveway and got out of her car. Tom was looking up to the sky and immediately Susan knew what was up.

"Hi, Susan," Tom said affably, "Thanks for coming so quickly. Look, I know that this is weird, but can you see that crow up there?" He pointed to the CSIS drone, "Well, it's not a crow at all. Rose and I think that it's some sort of surveillance drone. What do you think?"

And there lay the problem, Susan thought. Should she let Rose and Tom in on the CSIS operation and if so, what would they do and how would they react? She made her decision and said to Tom, "Let's go inside, Tom. I've got something to tell you."

Ten minutes later, Rose got up from the cane chair in the sunroom and announced that she would make some coffee. It was more of a diversion as she really needed to think through the implications of what Susan had said.

How could CSIS be involved and why would they have even considered Tom and her as prime suspects in a double murder case? This had her feeling an odd mixture of fear and anger. Adding to it all, Susan had asked them to keep it to themselves and pretend not to know anything about the CSIS operation. For the hundredth time Rose wondered what on earth their friends Andre and Jan had been up to.

Rose returned to the sunroom with a tray of coffee and a plate of orange and cranberry scones. Susan and Tom were ensconced in deep conversation, and she could see by Tom's face that he was not at all happy.

"I want to go and confront the surveillance team presumably sitting in that black van parked around the corner. What right do they have to be watching us?"

"Now Tom, if anyone is going to confront them it will be me. Just leave it another day as I want to get my notes together to deliver something of interest to CSIS before we go charging in. Remember, none of us are supposed to even know about the CSIS involvement. Look, I promise you that we'll get to the bottom of this soon. Just be patient."

Rose put the tray down onto the coffee table. She handed out the cups and offered the scones.

"Susan, are you getting any closer to finding the motive for Andre and Jan's murder?"

"We are making some progress. I can't tell you too much right now, but information is coming in from Interpol. We are getting a clearer picture of Andre and Jan. Their daughter, Lora, is flying into London this afternoon and I'm hoping to be able to interview her then."

"Where is she going to stay?" Rose asked, "Because she is more than welcome to stay with us. In fact, I insist that she comes here as that is the very least that we could do. You know, Susan, Jan and Andre were good people. I'm sure that they have been wrongfully murdered."

Susan nodded in agreement. "I think that it would be really good for Lora to stay with you. I'll let her know. She only has the one day to see her parents before going back to New York and, unfortunately, we cannot release their bodies until the case is over. Now I must be getting back to work.

Remember you must pretend to know absolutely nothing about CSIS. Do not discuss this with anyone."

Rose looked closely at her friend. Susan seemed almost frightened, and she was certainly deeply shaken. She must have been seriously spooked by her chief. As she got up to leave Rose gave her a big hug.

"We're so glad you're living here in Bayfield. Now don't forget lunch on Sunday. Be careful, Susan. I do worry about you."

Susan felt oddly tearful. This case was seriously getting to her. Something had to give, and soon.

NINE

The next day Susan arrived at the Lion's Hall a good forty minutes before her team. She had spent a couple of hours there the previous day and had made up a chart of known facts starting with Rose and Tom's meeting with Andre and Jan on safari in Kenya.

March - Rose and Tom meet Andre and Jan in Kenya
May 20 - Postcard from Andre and Jan postmarked May 10th and sent from New York
May 20 - Andre and Jan check into the Hampton Inn, Niagara
May 21st - Rose Blair discovers body of Jan at the marina. Andre checks into the Hessenland Inn
May 22nd - Andre found dead on Pavillion Road.

Susan glanced at her computer. Yesterday she had received a detailed forensics report on Andre Du Preez. The bullet extracted from his body matched that used to kill his wife. What was interesting, however, was the type of bullet most commonly used in North Korea and was manufactured in China. Analysis showed the unique blend of alloy metals used in the making of the bullets was only used in the Far East. *Interesting*, Susan thought, as she scrolled through the report. There was something cosmopolitan about the case, a South African couple murdered in Canada by a North Korean gun and Chinese made bullet.

CSIS'S INTEREST in the case only seemed to compound the issue further. Why would Canadian Security be at all involved unless there was an actual risk of terrorism? Thinking about CSIS made Susan remember the drone. She would have to get hold of those surveillance videos, as they could shed some light on the comings and goings at the Blair house.

The rest of the team arrived at 8:00 a.m., nearly all of them carrying Shop Bike coffees. Susan had made a pot of coffee before the meeting, but it looked like she would be the only person drinking it.

"Right, good morning," she said when everyone had settled down. "Let's have your reports as I'm sure you would like to go off and enjoy what's left of this beautiful Saturday morning. Constables Elliot and Brown, what have you to report?"

Constable Brown stood up, coughed, and then rummaged through his pocket and pulled out a notebook.

"Well, we started by interviewing people staying at The Cottage Colony. There were only two cabins booked then, although I believe they are solidly booked for the holiday weekend. Both couples in the two cabins drew a blank as no one had seen anything out of the ordinary. However, Constable Elliot spoke to the owner of the boat chandlery, and he remembered seeing a white Camry pull into the car park by the Cottage Colony and saw a woman get out, wave to the driver who then drove off. He said that she proceeded to walk down in the direction of the docks.

Now this is the interesting part. Minutes later he saw another car pull up, a grey Hyundai with New York license plates. The windows were tinted so he couldn't get a good look at the driver or the passenger. He did say that he thought the occupants were two men both with dark hair. The telephone rang in the shop and so he went back inside but not before hearing a car door slam. The next time he stepped out of the shop there was no sign of the car. That's all we have to report, Ma'am."

"Thank you, Constables. We have at last got a lead. A grey Hyundai with New York license plates, driven by a dark-haired man with a dark-haired male passenger. Not much to go on, but it's a start. Now Sergeant Mathieson, anything to report?"

The Sergeant stood up and pulled out his iPhone.

"Yes, Ma'am, a Stephen Clark was walking his dog when a grey car almost ran him over. The driver was driving like a maniac down Pavillion Road. All he could see were two people outlined in the tinted glass windows. He thought that they had black hair but couldn't swear on it. That is all, Ma'am."

Susan smiled. "Well, team, it looks like we might have found our assassins, now we just have to track down this grey car. One important item appears to be the bullets used to kill both Jan and Andre Du Preez.

"According to the forensics report, the metals used to make those bullets are only found in the Far East. During the Vietnam War, when thousands of bullets were manufactured, this combination of alloys was most commonly used as it was cheap and effective. Nowadays there appear to be only two countries in the world that manufacture this particular type of bullet, China and North Korea.

"Now the driver and passenger of the grey car have been identified as having dark hair. I know that this is a huge leap of faith, but maybe our assassins are either Chinese or Korean? I am going to dig a bit deeper with our friends from Interpol and see if Andre and Jan had any connections to our Asian friends. Also, Sergeant, could you check back with Border Control at Buffalo? It could be that the grey car followed the Du Preez's all the way from New York, otherwise how would they know where to find them?"

Sergeant Mathieson stood up and looked a little awkward. He cleared his throat before saying, "Well, with all due respect, Ma'am, the Blair's knew the Du Preez's were coming to Bayfield. In fact, they appear to have been connected all the way along. Do you not think that it is just too much of a coincidence that Rose Blair should discover the body of the first victim, Jan Du Preez, on their boat, and then, two days later, Tom should conveniently find the murdered husband, Andre? You are always telling us that you don't believe in coincidences, so I say that we should be keeping an eye on the Blairs. In my mind, they should still be on our list of suspects, if not for the actual killings, then for some sort of collaboration."

Susan thought about what the Chief had said about CSIS keeping up a surveillance on Rose and Tom and how they perceived the Blair's as suspects. She answered the Sergeant crisply. "We will keep an open mind, Sergeant, but to be quite blunt, to even suspect the Blair's of anything illegal seems to me ridiculous. Yes, I know that they are my friends, but you of all people should know just how much Rose has helped us in the past with other murder investigations. We will remain vigilant to the potential for collusion, but don't hold your breath. Right now, we need to gather more facts.

"The grey car has been identified as being a Hyundai with New York license plates, but the identity of the driver is still not known. However, I will pursue the possible Asian connection through Interpol. Right, we will meet again the same time tomorrow. Actually, there will be many people in the village for the town wide garage sale, plus the fact that it is the holiday weekend. After our briefing tomorrow, I want you all out on the streets interviewing people. Someone, somewhere will have seen the grey car and its occupants."

The team left the Lions Hall and Susan was just about to leave when her cell phone rang. It was Lora Du Preez calling to let Susan know that she would be arriving in London at three that afternoon.

Susan looked at her watch and realized that it was only 10:30. Enough time to put in a couple of hours work before leaving for London. She would take Lora to see her parents at the hospital morgue and afterwards she would drive her back to Bayfield where she would drop her off at Rose and Tom's to spend the night. Susan phoned Rose.

"Hi Rose. I've just heard from Lora Du Preez. She's arriving this afternoon and I'm meeting her at the airport and then taking her to see her parents. By the time we've done all of that and driven back to Bayfield, it's going to be close to 7:00 pm. Could I bring her around to you then or do you have other plans?"

"Well, that would be fine, Susan. How long will she be staying, as I've got all the family coming for lunch on Sunday, and don't forget that you've also been invited."

Susan replied quickly, "Don't worry, Rose, I think that Lora's only planning to stay one night. She originally had planned to be away a couple of days, but she has plans for Sunday back in the city. I'll drive her to the airport tomorrow afternoon."

Susan thought how convenient it was as she was already planning to drive to London for her date with Peter Joyce. Thinking about him made Susan smile. She had to ask Rose to repeat what she was saying.

"Are you sure that you're okay, Susan, you just sound a bit vague?"

"Oh, no, I'm just fine, Rose. I've just got a lot on my mind at the moment. Look, I'll see you later this evening."

Rose put the phone down and went into the kitchen where Tom was busy unloading the dishwasher. He looked up from what he was doing and said, "What's up, love? You look deep in thought."

"Oh, it's nothing really. That was Susan on the phone, and she sounded quite preoccupied."

"Well, that's not surprising, love, is it? She's in the middle of a double homicide. Talking of which, weren't we supposed to be going around to Lena's to get back your little red suitcase?"

Rose fairly jumped up. She had completely forgotten about her promise to Lena. Fortunately, the town wide garage sale wasn't until the following day, but it was just as well that Tom had remembered.

"Oh, Tom, let's go over to Lena's right now. We can walk the dogs so we will kill two birds with one stone."

Tom smiled wryly. Any mention of killing did not sit well with him at all.

TEN

Lora Du Preez was an attractive woman. She stood out in the crowd of people walking through the arrivals gate at London Airport. Susan waved to her and walked over to where she stood with a small travelling case in hand. Up closer, Susan could see how the news of her parent's deaths had devastated the poor woman. She could see it in her eyes and in the grim set of her mouth.

"Hi Lora. I'm Susan Parker, Detective Parker. How was your flight?"

Lora spoke with a soft South African accent and her voice, although quiet, showed strength and determination. What she said to Susan substantiated her air of inner strength and fortitude.

"You will get to the bottom of this, won't you Inspector? My parents were good people, and they did not deserve to die so horribly."

Susan reassured Lora that they were making some headway, but they were still trying to piece together a complete picture of her parents' movements prior to their deaths.

"It's a bit like doing a jig-saw," Susan explained, "Piecing together bits of information. You can help us a lot, Lora. Our biggest problem is trying to find a motive for their murders. Someone, somewhere cold heartedly planned these assassinations."

Lora sat impassively in the passenger seat of the car and for the longest time Susan thought that she had gone mute. She finally let out a deep sigh before saying, "Mom and dad rarely spoke about their past and the last time that we had a conversation about it they made me promise not to tell anyone." She blew her nose and sniffed a bit before continuing.

"You see, my mom was Jewish. Her maiden name was Isaacs. Her parents, my grandparents, both died at Auschwitz and my mother was raised by her one surviving sister, my Aunt Clara, who emigrated to South Africa after the war. My mother grew up a practicing Jew. She went to Jo'burg University where she met my dad. After they graduated, they went to Israel where they both worked on a Kibbutz for a year."

Susan thought for a minute. "But why did they make you promise not to talk about their early life?"

Lora blew her nose again.

"I don't think my mother wanted anyone to know about her Jewish background. After my mom and dad moved and settled in Windhoek, they had me and never embraced any religion. I was raised an atheist."

"What did your parents actually do, work wise, in Windhoek?"

"You know something, Susan, they were always very vague about their work. They worked at De Beers, and I know that they were both head-hunted from university. My mom has a doctorate in spectrum numerical patterning and my dad has a doctorate in systems analysis. They were very well respected in their fields. It is beyond me why anyone would want to murder them."

Susan glanced at Lora and could see her face scrunched up with emotion.

"Do you want to stop off at Tim Horton's before we head for the hospital? I know that I'm about ready for a coffee."

She pulled into the Tim Horton's around the corner from the hospital and they both went inside for coffee. Susan just knew that they were in for an ordeal and wanted to give the poor mourning daughter time to collect herself.

ELEVEN

Tom and Rose found Lena sorting through tables of items for the garage sale. She was sticking little price tags on different pieces. As they approached the table Lena looked up and smiled brightly.

"I don't know why I bother to price things as I mostly end up practically giving the stuff away. So, you're looking for your red suitcase?"

Rose glanced around and saw a pile of cases stacked to the back of the garage. She immediately spotted her old red case missing a wheel.

"Ah, I can see it, Lena. Do you mind if we take it back home, we'll get it back to you when we're finished?"

Lena looked at Rose and Tom speculatively before saying. "I suppose you're not going to tell me what's going on? I know you two, something's cooking."

Rose smiled and patted Lena on her shoulder.

"Thanks, Lena, I'll return this tomorrow."

With that Rose and Tom left and walked back home. As they trundled down Colina Street, they noticed the black van parked by the sidewalk. All the windows were tinted so they were unable to see anyone or anything inside.

"Tom, I wish that we hadn't promised Susan not to confront them. I hope that she speaks to them soon otherwise I will knock on that van door personally and demand to know what they are doing. It's an invasion of our privacy and I don't like it one single bit."

They had reached Bayfield Terrace and Puff and Ben lurched forward tugging at their leashes. Rose unclipped them a few metres from the house and both dogs charged forward to the front door.

Tom carried the red case into the living room. He opened it and peered inside. There was nothing but the black, silk lining. Rose walked over and also peered into the empty void.

"Maybe there's something tucked into the lining," she said while feeling the sides and bottom of the case with her hands. Suddenly she stopped and patted an area of lining at the side of the case. "Tom, feel just here. Doesn't it feel lumpy to you?"

Tom ran his fingers over the inside lining and stopped where Rose had, groping his fingers around the raised up area gently.

"Rose, get me a pair of scissors, there's definitely something here. I need to cut into the lining."

Rose hurried off to the kitchen and returned with a pair of scissors. Soon Tom had slit the lining and pulled out a folded sheet of paper. On the paper were four typed columns of numbers.

"Gosh, more numbers, Tom. What on earth do they mean?"

"Well, I don't know, love, but I'm going to compare these numbers with the other set of numbers written on that scrap of paper I found on Andre. They must mean something. Do you think that we should hand them over to Susan?"

"No, not yet, Tom. I reckon these numbers have to be pretty significant to be hidden in the lining of my case. Which, you realize, means that Andre and Jan must have premeditated all of this intentionally, using us as mules."

"Oh, they probably just befriended us purposely to get these numbers out of the country, but what I don't understand is if they were travelling to the U.S.A. anyway to visit their daughter, why bother to hide the numbers with us when they could have just as easily taken them out of the country themselves."

Rose frowned, "But that still begs the question, why go to the trouble of hiding these numbers in the first place? Oh Tom, this all seems terribly confusing. I'm going to make us a nice cup of tea and then I'm going to really study these numbers and see if there is some sort of pattern to them."

TWELVE

Susan and Lora drove back to Bayfield in complete silence. Seeing her parents lying in the hospital morgue had knocked the stuffing out of both women. Lora had been visibly shaken with distress when they had wheeled out the trolley and pulled back the sheets. Susan had to put her arms around her and lead her away sobbing her heart out.

They had arrived at Rose and Tom's house only to be greeted effusively by Ben and Puff. Ben rushed out just as Tom opened the door to a rather startled Lora. Susan grabbed hold of Ben's collar and led him back inside.

"So sorry," Tom said as he took hold of Ben, "He's not usually quite so boisterous. I hope you don't mind dogs. They're very much a part of our lives. By the way, I'm Tom and you must be Lora?"

Tom extended his hand to shake Lora's. She looked noticeably more relaxed and when she smiled Tom couldn't help himself saying, "Oh, my, you look so much like your mother." To which Lora's face crumpled and large tears started to roll down her cheeks, Tom looked horrified. "Oh, I'm so very sorry. How very tactless of me. Please come inside and meet my wife, Rose."

Susan paused on the doorstep.

"I won't come in, Tom, but I'll swing by in the morning. We've already set a time for Lora to leave Bayfield. Her plane leaves early tomorrow afternoon, around 3:00 p.m. I'll pick her up at about 12:30 p.m., if that's okay?"

Rose greeted Lora with a big hug and showed her the way to the guest bedroom.

Looking at the young woman standing nervously in the lobby, she reminded Rose a little of Jessica, their daughter. She would be roughly the same age, probably in her late thirties and very attractive. What an awful ordeal for her to have gone through having to identify her parents in a morgue. Rose shuddered at the mere thought and took Lora's hand in sympathy.

Rose spoke gently to Lora, "Dinner will be in about half an hour and then we might go for a little walk around the village. It's such a beautiful evening and it will be still light until around 8:30 p.m. I'll leave you to freshen up."

Rose went back to the kitchen and continued to prepare their evening meal. She had decided to make a South African meal in honour of their guest. She would make Babootie and serve that with roasted vegetables and potatoes with a tossed salad.

For dessert she had made a mango mousse. There was a small, crusty loaf of artisan bread with herb butter.

"Tom, could you lay the table, please?"

Rose called out to Tom who had disappeared off to sit in the sunroom. Puff and Ben had followed him and were both curled up on the sofa alongside Tom.

Lora appeared five minutes later just as Tom was putting out the wine glasses and cutlery for dinner. She looked visibly more refreshed and had even changed into a loose fitting, brightly coloured kaftan.

"Can I help you, Rose?" she said with her soft South African accent.

"No, my dear, it's all done. Would you like a glass of wine or something else? Maybe a gin and tonic?"

Lora opted for the wine, while Rose and Tom both sipped on large gin and tonics. They led the way to the sunroom where Puff and Ben were still sleeping.

"Puff, Ben. Off the sofa." Rose said.

"They're really spoilt, but we love them to pieces. We'll have our drinks in here before eating. It's all ready but can wait a while. I want to hear all about life in New York."

Lora sat down and sighed before saying, "This is so kind of you and your house is lovely. You know something, the saddest thing of all is I had such a good time with mom and dad when they visited. It's unbelievable to think that it was only a week ago. No, I won't cry anymore, I'm all cried out, but I just can't stop thinking about how happy they seemed and so full of life. Mom looked really well. Did you know that she had had a brush with cancer last year?"

Rose looked surprised and answered, "Gosh, no, she never said anything to me at all. I had no idea that she had been ill."

"Yes, well, she put such a brave face on it and refused to let it get her down. She certainly seemed to have got her old energy back. I took the week off work and showed them all the sights and we walked for miles and miles. They were both so excited to actually be in New York. We had a wonderful time together." Lora paused as she reflected on her time with her parents. Suddenly she jumped up saying," Oh, I completely forgot, I have something for you. My father gave it to me just before they left. It's in my suitcase, I'll just go and get it."

Lora got up and left the sunroom. Rose looked at Tom and raised her eyebrows.

"What on earth could Andre have left with Lora to give to us? Anyhow, how would he even know that she would be seeing us?"

Before Tom could answer Lora had returned holding a thin, white envelope. Rose and Tom's names were clearly written on the front. Tom opened it quickly. He pulled out a single sheet of paper upon which were four columns with numbers in each column. At first glance it looked almost identical to the other sheet of paper extracted from the lining of the suitcase. On closer inspection, however, Tom just knew that the numbers were different.

Rose asked Lora the question that both Tom and she really wanted answered,

"Lora what exactly did your father say when he gave you this envelope to give to us?"

Lora answered quietly. "He said that if anything happened to Mom and him you were to be given this envelope. My dad said that you would know what to do with it."

Tom handed her the piece of paper and Lora looked at the sheet of numbers and gave a mirthless laugh.

"Oh, that's so typical of my parents. They were always leaving encrypted codes for me to decipher. I swear that I was the only girl in my school who had to break a code in order to find out where her birthday presents were hidden. I actually got quite good at deciphering."

Tom smiled and gave Rose a meaningful look. He got up and went to the study where he unlocked the drawer and pulled out the two sheets of paper, one that was found on Andre's body and the other, inside the suitcase lining. The one from Andre contained only one line of numbers and the single word TAS, whereas the other two sheets of paper had four columns of numbers. Tom carried them over to Lora.

"Well, Lora, see if you can make sense of these." And he handed her the papers.

Lora frowned but bent her head closer and started to scrutinize the codes.

THIRTEEN

After Susan had dropped Lora off, she decided to go for dinner at The Docks. As she pulled into the car park Susan noticed a grey car, a Hyundai, carrying New York number plates. She got out her notebook and wrote down the license number.

During dinner she looked around the restaurant trying to see if there were two dark haired men. There were several men with dark hair, but they were accompanied by women. Susan was about to place her order when, out of the window, she noticed the grey car pull out and drive off. She jumped up, grabbed her car keys, and dashed out of the restaurant to where her car was parked.

It had been many years since she had been involved in a car chase and she knew that she should immediately call for back up, but there was no time. The grey Hyundai turned left onto the highway and then headed North in the direction of Goderich. Susan followed cautiously; she didn't know if the driver knew if he was being followed. They passed The Ashwood on the right and then without indicating, the Hyundai sped up, overtaking the car in front and then took a sharp right onto Bayfield Road to Clinton.

Susan gripped her steering wheel and put her foot down on the accelerator. The chase was on, as the driver had obviously clocked her.

He suddenly turned left onto Orchard Line. Susan just made it in time with screeching wheels her car narrowly missed a sign for the Stonefield Garden Centre. They sped past the Berry Farm not stopping at the stop sign by Pine Lake. This is crazy, thought Susan as they raced past Cut Line Road. Suddenly, the Hyundai braked and did a 'U' turn almost right in front of Susan causing her to swing right over onto the verge for fear of crashing. By the time she had stopped and turned the car around, the grey car had managed to gain enough distance that Susan knew it would prove impossible to catch up. She grabbed her car radio and called for help giving the car's license plate number and model.

With a sinking heart, Susan drove back to Bayfield. Her stomach grumbled reminding her that she had not eaten. She would return to The Docks and have that intended meal. Just maybe one of the servers might remember seeing the two dark haired men, although Susan knew that she was probably chasing rainbows.

FOURTEEN

After their dinner Rose, Tom, and Lora retired to the sunroom where Tom poured them all some wine. Over their meal they had reminisced about the safari and how they had enjoyed getting to know Lora's parents. Lora talked about growing up in Windhoek and how she had won a scholarship to study in Washington and then stayed on to do her doctorate at NYU. She talked about working for the UN and how demanding the work was and how she would just love to return to Namibia where her heart lay and where the lifestyle was more relaxed, and the sun shone all year around.

"I will have to go back to Windhoek to settle up my parents' affairs and to sell the house, although maybe I could keep it." She said wistfully.

Lora looked sad and then her face crumpled.

"Oh, my, gosh, I completely forgot about Rusty and Riley my parents two Rhodesian Ridgebacks. Mom and dad boarded them in kennels while they were away. Oh, I can't just leave them there. The kennel owners will have them put down. Oh no, this is awful." And she began to softly cry. Rose put her arms around Lora and said quietly.

"I'm sure that the dogs will be okay, but I do think that you need to go back and sort out your parent's affairs. Don't make any hasty decisions yet, Lora. Maybe you might find someone who could look after Rusty and Riley or you could even have them flown back with you to New York. Right now, you need time to mourn the loss of your mom and dad.

"Look, before you leave telephone or email the kennels and ask them if they would board the dogs for a couple more weeks and then you could ask your boss if you could take some compassionate leave. They will understand, I'm sure."

Tom smiled to himself. There Rose was at it again, micro-managing Lora's life. She couldn't help it; she was just a natural manager of people.

Before they all turned in for the night Lora said to Tom. "Oh, by the way, I think that I've broken the code on the small piece of paper. Corinthians 1, chapter 13, verses 4 to 13. That's typical of dad, he often used Biblical references. Do you have a copy of the Bible handy? I'll need it to decode the two pages of the numbers."

Tom went to his study and returned with the King James version of the Bible. With that accomplished they all went to bed.

FIFTEEN

S usan was woken from a deep sleep by her cell phone ringing insistently. It was Sergeant Mathieson.

"Ma'am, sorry to disturb you at this early hour, but I thought that you would like to know that we found the grey Hyundai abandoned just up from the Ben Miller Inn on Black Point Road. Forensics are busy dusting it for fingerprints. We're certain that this is the same car reported leaving the crime scene on Pavillion Road and the same car that you gave chase to last night."

"Thank you, Sergeant," Susan said as she glanced at her bedside clock. It was only 5:00 a.m. *I might as well get up now,* Susan thought as she padded downstairs to the kitchen to make some coffee. Twenty minutes later Susan left her condo and went for a run. She decided to run up to Jowetts Grove and then back along the Highway down to the docks and then back up the hill to the Harbour Court condos. It would still give her time to shower and dress before going to the Lions Hall for the team meeting.

At 8:00 a.m. the team were all gathered, once again with Shop Bike coffees in their hands. Susan had dressed in an emerald green skirt with a paler green peasant blouse. She had spent a bit of extra time on her appearance as she wouldn't have time to change before her date with Peter Joyce after taking Lora to the London airport.

He had said he would cook dinner, Indian if she liked, as that was his favourite. Susan loved the thought of a man cooking for her. Henri didn't even know how to fry an egg let alone cook a meal. In all her previous relationships the men had just taken her out to dinner. Susan so looked forward to the dinner and a small shiver of anticipation shot through her body at the thought of what might lie ahead.

"Well, good morning everyone, and a beautiful one at that. So, let's be having your reports. Sergeant, you can go first."

Sergeant Mathieson stood up.

"The grey Hyundai was found at 4:30 a.m. this morning abandoned on Black Point Road. Border Services have the same vehicle checking through immigration on May 19th, the same day as Andre and Jan Du Preez. In fact, they entered Canada at the same entry point exactly ten minutes later. The license plates on the car are registered to Hertz rental in the US. Border Services report that the two occupants were indeed Korean, Minjaan Kim and Jejoon Jihur with addresses in North Korea. Immigration say that the names and passports are probably false, but they can do facial imaging and right now they have sent their photos to be scanned into their facial recognition software. Interpol will then do a search for us. If they have a criminal record, we will know about it soon. That is all I have to report, Ma'am."

Susan thanked the Sergeant. "Now it appears that Windhoek has just sent a report of a break in at the Du Preez residence last night. The house was torn apart as if someone was looking for something specific. The computers were stolen yet friends who knew the Du Preez's were asked to look at the contents of the house to see if they could recall anything missing and other than the computers, everything else was left intact.

"Apparently, according to the police report of break and entries, the Du Preez's had previously been burgled last March when the couple were away on safari. It was the same pattern then with only computers stolen and nothing else. Now team, it looks like the Du Preez's were followed from New York to Bayfield by two Koreans driving a grey Hyundai which now has been found abandoned near Ben Miller on Black Point Road. The fact that these men took the trouble to follow them all the way from New York indicates that the Du Preez's must have either had something of great significance to them or were headed towards something important.

"Sergeant Mathieson, I am giving you the task of finding out just who these Koreans are and what it is they are after. Work with Interpol and leave no stone unturned. Constables Brown and Elliot we need to find these two Koreans and fast. They haven't disappeared into thin air. It is possible that they might try to leave the country so inform Border Services. They need to be found and quickly. We now have the means and the opportunity, but we still don't have the motive. Right, men, keep digging, something will surface I'm sure, I feel that we are getting closer, but we don't want this case growing cold on us."

The team left soon afterwards leaving Susan to type up her report to the Chief. She looked at her watch and realized that it was only 10:30 a.m. She still had time to speak to Tom and Rose before taking Lora to London to catch her flight back to New York.

SIXTEEN

Lora appeared much more relaxed at the breakfast table than she had been the night before. She laughingly claimed that she had been up most of the night trying to crack the code her parents had left. Although the Corinthian verse was the guide, her father had made it even more complicated by reversing the number connotation. Over a frittata with bacon and sausages, fresh orange juice and artisan bread, Lora told Rose and Tom what she had deciphered.

"You see, if I use the passage from Corinthians 1, chapter 13, verse 4 to 13, as a guide the numbers refer to the words. For instance, in this column," she held up one of the pieces of paper with four columns of numbers, "the first number 6 refers to the sixth letter in the Corinthians verse which in this case is an S. It's a painfully slow process and I'm very sorry as I'm still only halfway through the exercise. I'll work on it a bit more later on if that's okay by you."

"Oh, Lora, thank you so much. Tom told me that you were using that lovely verse from Corinthians. They recite that so often at weddings, 'Love is patient, love is kind. It does not envy, it does not boast, it is not proud'... and so it goes on. I always cry a bit when I hear it read out. It was recited beautifully at my friend Mary Stokes' funeral."

Rose went a bit quiet as she remembered vividly the day she had found her friend Mary slumped over a gravestone in the Bayfield Cemetery just behind the Croquet Club.

She sniffed and coughed and then continued saying,

"Now, enough of my maudlin thoughts. It's such a beautiful morning and we never did have that walk last night. How about we leave clearing away the breakfast things and go for a walk right now. It's our town wide garage sale today so you never know, you might even find a treasure to take back to New York with you."

Rose, Tom, Lora, and the dogs left soon afterwards and headed for the beach. Lora left the slip of paper with the deciphered Corinthians verse lying on the coffee table.

It was a truly amazing morning with a clear sky and crystal blue water. On days like this Rose felt good to be alive and so blessed to be living in the beautiful village of Bayfield.

They walked to Pioneer Park, and she explained to Lora how the park was actually owned by an association like a board of trustees and how this group of very well-meaning people were guardians of the park so that nobody could ever destroy the beauty of it. Looking out over the lake from the top of the stairs Lora was amazed at how the lake looked like the ocean.

Coming from New York which looked out over the Atlantic Ocean, she remarked that she had never known that the Great Lakes were so massive although she had read somewhere that the lakes constituted one of the largest fresh water supplies in the whole world. They then all three walked down the steps to the beach.

Even though it was just 10:00 a.m. already some keen sailors were out and about in their boats. They walked to the pier and looked out over the marina. Over on the north shore Rose could see a sleek, black power boat moored on the dock further up from *Tranquility*. It was the same boat that she had seen before and there was something rather sinister about it. Maybe it was the antennae and small satellite dish on top of the cabin, but it made Rose shiver.

Puff and Ben had made a bee line for the water and, although Tom tried to call them back, they were both swimming before he could stop them. The trouble with wet dogs was that they got very smelly and on top of that invariably one of them would end up rolling in a dead fish which would compound the smell further. *Oh well,* Tom thought, he would have to just hose them down before they were let back in the house again. They put both dogs back on their leashes and walked back up Long Hill to Bayfield Terrace. When they reached their house Tom looked at Rose quizzically.

"Did you leave the front door open, love?"

Rose looked horrified.

"No, of course I did not. Oh Tom, don't say that we've been broken into again and before you ask, no, I did not lock up either, I thought that you had."

They all tentatively approached the house. Tom made the women stay back while he went inside with the dogs. Shortly afterwards he appeared giving them the thumbs up sign,

"Doesn't look like anything has been disturbed. Can you see if something is missing, love?"

Rose looked around the house and then Lora let out a shriek.

"The piece of paper with the decoded Corinthians passage, it's gone. I left it on the coffee table, well, look, it's not there anymore."

Rose and Tom looked around the living room, but there was no sign of the piece of paper.

"Lora, what about the other sheets of paper with the columns of numbers. Have they gone too?"

Rose and Tom looked so relieved when Lora pulled them out of her jacket pocket.

"Here they are, it's my force of habit I'm afraid, I automatically fold papers up and stuff them in my pockets."

"Oh, my, gosh, thank goodness for habits. Well, at least we know that those papers are important. The burglar won't get far with the Corinthians verse, in fact, I bet he's puzzling over it right now." Rose said as she looked anxiously out of the window.

"Tom, do you think that we should call Susan?"

As if on cue, Susan's car pulled into the driveway.

"Tom, did you just call her? Well, are we going to own up to not locking the house again or do we not tell her anything?"

Lora looked at Rose and Tom questionably. Tom quickly said to them both. "Let's just keep this break in to ourselves shall we, otherwise we will have to tell her about the coded papers and until Lora's deciphered them, I'd rather keep it to ourselves."

Susan knocked on the door and Puff and Ben charged, tails wagging as they already knew who it was. They adored Susan.

Rose opened the door.

"Gosh, you're lucky to find us in, Susan, we've just returned from a lovely walk. Isn't it a wonderful day?"

"It sure is. Did you sleep alright, Lora?" Susan asked as she followed Rose into the sitting room.

"I slept like a log. Oh, the village of Bayfield is adorable, it's so quaint. I'm sorry not to be able to spend longer here, maybe under different circumstances..." her voice trailed off as the sadness of her visit enveloped her once more.

Lora did look more rested and her whole body language appeared more relaxed.

"Rose and Tom, I just wanted to ask you a few questions. Rose, when you were down at the docks and," here Susan looked at Lora and said, "Sorry, Lora, you may not want to listen to this." She turned back to Rose and continued, "When you went to clean the boat, did you happen to notice a grey saloon car with tinted windows?"

Rose thought for a minute. She was useless at recognizing makes of cars, but could she remember even seeing any cars let alone a specific grey car down at the docks? She shook her head.

"No, Susan, all I remember was that there was absolutely nobody about. It was eerily quiet. No, I really cannot recall seeing any cars at all."

"Well, have you or Tom, seen a grey car around the village?"

Tom thought for a minute. Contrary to Rose he had a good eye and memory for cars.

"Yes, if I remember rightly, I saw a grey car, a Hyundai, parked on Colina Street just around the corner from Anne Street. I was taking stuff around to Lena's for the garage sale. That was yesterday around 2:00 p.m."

Susan wrote the time and date in her notebook.

"Now, Rose and Tom, it seriously looks as if the perpetrators are looking for something. We have just found out that the Du Preez, your parent's, home was burgled, and I believe," Susan turned to Lora, "they were also burgled last March when they were away on safari. Do you know anything about this? The police report says that only your parents' computers were stolen, nothing else."

Lora nodded, "Yes, I remember Mom was particularly distressed about it. Burglaries are pretty common in Windhoek, but this was so bizarre. It had them quite perplexed."

"And you both," Susan looked at Rose and Tom, "you had that mysterious break in when Puff and Ben were shut outside yet nothing was stolen. It all points to someone searching for something. We just don't know what it is?"

Susan looked at her watch and said to Lora, "I'll just go and grab a bite to eat and then I'll be back to take you to the airport in about an hour. See you then."

Rose saw Susan to the front door and waved goodbye to her friend. She turned to Tom and said, "We really should have given her the pieces of paper with the numbers. Lora, how long will it take for you to decipher this? Maybe you should just show Tom and I what to do and then we could have ago this afternoon?"

Lora picked up the sheets of paper and glanced at them again.

"It is a painfully slow process you know. Look, I'll just guide you through it and once you know how the pattern works you will find it easy to do, just very slow."

The next half hour Tom, Rose, and Lora sat around the table the Bible open at the Book of Corinthians. Tom counted the letters of each sentence and cross referenced them with the chapter and verse in the Bible. Rose scribed. By the time Susan had returned an hour later, they were halfway through the decoding. Tom put the pieces of paper away in his desk.

It was an emotional farewell. In the short time they had got to know Lora, it now felt almost as if she was one of the family. Rose hugged her saying, "Stay in touch, Lora, you know where we are, please come and visit us soon."

As they drove off Tom got the papers out of the study and beckoned to Rose to continue the deciphering. The code had to be broken and then maybe they might understand more easily what was at stake.

SEVENTEEN

Susan drove Lora to the airport. It was a lovely sunny afternoon and the countryside looked particularly lush and green. Driving through Exeter and then Lucan, Susan thought about the many times she had driven the same route over the past four years. Before the murder on the beach in Bayfield, Susan had rarely travelled to the west coast of Ontario. She had mostly stayed and worked in London. Now she couldn't wait to leave the city and be back in the peaceful village which she now called home.

Lora appeared deep in thought for most of the journey and Susan felt that she probably needed the time to process everything that had happened over the past three days. The poor girl was now an orphan and with that came the onerous task of sorting out her parents' affairs. Susan hoped that the Du Preez's had a good lawyer back in Windhoek. She had a feeling that there would be much to sort through in her parent's estate.

Lora had told her that her friend and partner, Celia, would be meeting her at the airport in New York. It had come as a bit of a surprise to Susan that Lora was in a same sex relationship, but why it should have? Susan didn't quite know. She had several friends who were in similar relationships. Many of them had been in heterosexual relationships, some even married with children, before they had discovered their preference for the company of a same sex partner. *I suppose,* Susan thought looking over at Lora, *it was just my own preconception.* She was a young and attractive woman who could have had the pick of any man.

Susan pulled up in front of the departure lounge. She loved London Airport as it was small and easy to navigate. There was also a Tim Horton's right in the departure lounge. She did not however, park the car. In fact, had she been more observant, Susan would have seen a black sedan pull in behind her. As it was, she said her goodbyes to Lora, and drove off, keenly anticipating her date with Peter Joyce.

EIGHTEEN

The rich aroma of cardamom, coriander, garlic, cumin, and cinnamon greeted Susan at the door to Peter Joyce's house. The spices were so pungent that she could smell the curry all the way down the driveway. Susan rang the doorbell and Peter answered, welcoming her with a hug.

He was dressed casually in blue jeans and a crisp, white shirt open at the neckline with his sleeves rolled up. Susan immediately noticed his bare feet. *Nice toes,* she thought while removing her own sandals and entering the lobby.

She had been to his house once before last year, so she felt comfortable taking off her jacket and walking into the open plan living room. Covering the walls were magnificent photographs taken from all over the world. Peter had explained that once upon a time, in a different life, he had worked for National Geographic, hence all the amazing photographs from around the globe.

Norah Jones was playing softly in the background and Susan noticed an old fashioned 70s style record deck, amplifier and speakers set up in the living room.

A stack of vinyl records rested in a rack to one side of the stone fireplace. Susan loved vinyl. She'd kept all of her vinyl records dating back to the early 70s. In her collection she had records by The Beatles, Rolling Stones, Carpenters, The Beach Boys, Joni Mitchell, Carli Simon, Simon and Garfunkel, as well as many other lesser-known artists. Peter interrupted her train of thought.

"I never did ask you if there was anything you didn't like to eat?"

Susan laughed and said that she wasn't fussy, she ate most things although she wasn't too keen on lobster, crab, snails, mussels, and generally anything in a shell.

"Don't worry, I've steered clear of fish. Do you know that the levels of mercury found in large fish, is dreadfully high? You're alright eating the small fish like sardines, but these days I don't ever touch the big fish."

Susan had read about the mercury levels in fish in a MacLean's magazine just the other day. It had quite shocked her and had quite put her off eating tuna fish in particular. But the worst thing that she read was about the increased quantity of plastic beads in the oceans, so microscopic that the eye could barely see them. These were ingested by fish and contained carcinogens which, when consumed by man, could contribute to cancer. The plastics beads were the direct result of long-term accumulations of plastics discarded in the waterways by man, mostly in the form of plastic bottles and bags, and were in effect rapidly destroying the water quality not only in the world's oceans, but also in the Great Lakes.

"Are you an environmentalist, Peter?"

He laughed in an easy-going manner.

"Well, I believe in global warming and am continually horrified by man's ignorance and complete disregard for nature, just don't get me started. Now, what can I get you to drink? White wine, gin and tonic, or beer, you name it and I've probably got it."

Susan asked for a glass of white wine and then went to sit on one of the leather sofas. His living room was pretty minimalist and very masculine. Two black ultra-modern leather sofas faced each other, and a square glass and stainless-steel coffee table sat between them on a black and white striped carpet.

A grey, slate stone fireplace rose from the floor to the ceiling and a beautifully framed black and white photograph of what looked like Tibet with mountains souring to the sky hung on the stone fireplace. Suddenly Susan felt very unworldly and the urge to travel tugged at her heart strings.

"You must have visited nearly every country in the world, Peter?"

Peter handed Susan a glass of white chardonnay and then sat down on the sofa beside her.

"Yes, well the world is so small, and you only have one life. But you know, Susan, I'm tired of all that travelling. I used to keep a packed bag by the front door because I never would know when the next assignment would be and where I would be going. I got burnt out after twenty years of living that nomadic style of life. Now, I'm happy freelancing and doing police work when needed; and it pays the bills."

Susan was quiet while she digested this information. Peter had not mentioned an ex-wife or anything about past relationships, but she thought that having a husband forever flying off on some photographic shoot or another would not have been very conducive to a good relationship.

"Right, now dinner is pretty well ready. Would you like to come and sit up?"

Susan followed Peter to a beautifully laid table. The cloth looked Eastern with finely woven red, gold, and blue threads. In the middle of the table was a large ebony elephant about one foot tall.

"Wow, that's a beautiful carving, Peter. Where did you get it?"

Peter gently picked up the elephant. He held it tightly against his chest and Susan could see that it held some deep emotional significance to him.

"I got it when I was on a photo shoot in Zaire. I rarely buy souvenirs, but I couldn't resist this one."

"Tell me, Peter, is there anywhere that you haven't visited?" Susan asked while sitting up at the table.

"Oh, yes, there are plenty of places in the world left to visit and whether I get to them or not doesn't in the least bit bother me. I have enough memories of all the other places I've been to last me a lifetime. Now, do you want a top up or switch to a red wine with your meal?"

Susan chose to stick with the chardonnay and sat back ready to enjoy the evening. First, Peter served a cluster of tiny samosas served on a bed of lettuce with a spoonful of mango chutney to one side. There was warm naan bread in a basket. Susan bit into one of the delicate samosas. They were perfect with just the right amount of spice to give them a bit of a kick but not hot enough to leave her mouth on fire.

Next Peter served butter chicken and a lentil dahl for the main course with a bowl of fragrant jasmine rice. It was all absolutely delicious. Susan couldn't help using the naan bread to mop up the last drop of sauce from her plate.

"That was heavenly." She said as Peter started to clear away the plates.

"I'm afraid I don't do desserts, but there are wedges of melon and I have a plate of chocolate cookies. Would you like some coffee?"

While Peter put the coffee on and cleared away the table, Susan looked at the photographs on the wall once more. Peter was such a talented photographer although it was obvious that human interest pictures were not his forte. Which was a shame because Susan just loved photographs with children of different ethnicities depicted in their own cultures and traditions.

Afterwards, Peter joined Susan in the living room putting the tray of coffee down on the glass topped coffee table. He sat down on the sofa next to Susan and poured out the coffee. The very closeness of him made Susan catch her breath.

She could almost feel his body heat and smell his sensuality. Suddenly Susan just knew that she wanted him and couldn't wait any longer. In profile his face looked even more handsome with his aquiline nose and strong chin. His eyes met hers and she smiled and opened her lips thinking to herself, *please kiss me, Peter, kiss me.* Peter slowly reached out and touched her face and with his thumb he traced her lips. Suddenly, his arms were around her and their lips met, and Susan felt that she would drown in his passion.

She pressed her body against his and then she was undoing his shirt buttons and pulling at his jeans. Before long they both lay naked on the sofa feeling each other and exploring the newness of each other with every inch of skin and contours of their bodies. Finally, they were as one and Susan came with such a rush of joy that she cried out, "Don't stop, Peter, oh don't stop." It was as if she had stored up all her sexual passion and now it had erupted like a volcano as she had been brought to explosive heights.

Afterwards Susan whispered, "My God, Peter, that was fantastic." And Peter just smiled as he took her hands and kissed them one finger at a time.

"It's not over yet," he said provocatively, and he proceeded to pick her up and carry her through to his bedroom where their love making started all over again - this time slower, more tender, and infinitely more enduring.

. . .

IT WAS past 11:00 p.m. before Susan roused herself and realized the time.

"Peter, my darling, I really do have to go. We have a team meeting early tomorrow morning and then I've been invited over to Rose and Tom Blair's place for lunch. Tell me when we can see each other again?"

Peter clasped Susan's hand to his heart. His hair was all disheveled and he wore a lopsided grin on his boyishly handsome face.

"Could I come over to Bayfield tomorrow night?"

Susan grabbed his other hand and kissed his palm.

"Oh, please, yes, I'll be counting the hours. Now, don't get up, I'll take a quick shower and then I'll let myself out. See you, my darling, till tomorrow."

They kissed deeply again, and Peter tried his hardest to pull her back into bed, but Susan stopped him and left before she herself succumbed to his and her own desires.

Driving back to Bayfield Susan couldn't stop herself smiling. She hadn't felt so happy for over a year, at least not since Henri's death.

NINETEEN

Rose woke up with a start. It was eight o'clock and the kids would be arriving in just a few hours. Normally she would have had everything organized by now, but Tom and she had been up to well past midnight trying to make sense of the decoded numbers. They had followed Lora's directions but were left with a jumble of letters that made even more jumbled words. Finally, Tom had said that they should call it a day and go to bed.

All night Rose had been trying to make sense of the letters they had deciphered and now she had woken up in a panic. The family was coming. Lunch had to be prepared.

She left Tom still sleeping and went to make a pot of tea. Lying on the kitchen table were the sheets of papers with the decoded letters. Rose picked up the sheet of paper with what appeared to be nonsense words. She grabbed another blank piece of paper and covered over the first line of words. That didn't work, but it made Rose think. What if she were to take the first letter of each word and make words that way. Like a jigsaw, slowly proper words were formed and soon Rose had what looked like co-ordinates for a map. It read:

NW 123, OJ10K, RTZ.

But what OJ or RTZ meant was beyond Rose.

The telephone rang and Rose ran to answer it before Tom woke up. It was a rather worried sounding woman with a thick Brooklyn accent who introduced herself as "Celia, Lora's friend."

"Oh, Mrs. Blair, I'm so worried. I went to the airport expecting to meet Lora off the plane. She never arrived and I haven't heard from her. Do you know where she is?"

Rose stood there stock still. She knew that Susan would have dropped her off at the airport so what could have possibly happened to the poor girl? She would have to telephone Susan and maybe she would be able to shed some light on it.

Taking Celia's cell number and promising to get back as soon as she had some news, Rose said goodbye and phoned Susan. There was no answer. Rose thought for a minute. Likely Susan would be in the middle of one of her team meetings. She decided to send her a text message.

Call me straight away, urgent. Lora's gone missing.

While she waited for Susan to reply, Rose got out the ingredients to make choux pastry for the profiteroles that she had planned to bake for the family get together. Melting the butter in boiling water and then stirring in the flour and mixing it to a paste, soothed Rose's jagged nerves. She went to the fridge and got out a box of eggs. One by one she beat in four eggs until she had a smooth and silky paste. Often she piped the profiteroles, but this time she just used a teaspoon and dropped little golden mounds onto the parchment paper lined tray. Putting the baking tray in the preheated oven, Rose looked at the time. 8:40, she would make another pot of tea and bring a cup to Tom. It was time that he woke up and started the day.

Lora looked around the sparsely furnished living room. It was clean and comfortable enough and very IKEA, yet she still felt like a prisoner. The officer had assured her that she was in a 'safe' house and that there were police officers posted outside, but she didn't feel safe. All she wanted was to be back in New York in her own comfortable apartment.

After Susan had dropped her off at the airport she was just about to walk into the terminal when two suited men came up to her. At first, she thought that they might be Jehovah's Witnesses, but then one gently took her arm and the other pulled out his warrant card and introduced himself as CSIS Agent Roberts.

"Please could you come with us, ma'am," he had said very politely. Lora had meekly been led to their car where, before she knew what was happening, they had her sitting in the back seat and had driven off at a high speed.

She knew that they were in London, somewhere in an unknown city, they had driven past factories and then turned left next to something called The Western Fairground. She had demanded to know what was going on and why she was been taken to a safe house. In answer to all her questions Agent Roberts had told Lora to be patient, they would explain everything shortly, but not to be alarmed as it was all for her own good.

Meanwhile back in Bayfield, Rose paced the floor. Susan still had not replied. She had woken Tom up with the news of Lora's disappearance and, in his usual way, Tom had told her to calm down and stop worrying. There would be a simple explanation. Maybe Lora had flown to La Guardia airport and not JFK or even Newark? But Rose couldn't stop worrying as she felt that she owed it to Andre and Jan to look out for their daughter.

The profiteroles looked like little golden puffs. Rose busied herself making the confectioners custard to fill the choux pastry buns. She then made a chocolate sauce to pour over the finished puffs. Standing back Rose admired the little 'mountain' of chocolate coated profiteroles. Tom walked by and was about to absent-mindedly take one when Rose caught him in time.

"Tom, they're for our dessert. Look, you can have one of these." Rose handed him one of her rejects, a misshapen profiterole oozing with creamy custard.

"Yum, these are delicious, love. Now what can I do to help? Jessica will be here pretty soon, and you know how crazy it gets once Abby and Ella arrive."

Rose smiled. She loved their granddaughters to pieces and could hardly wait to see them again. In the summertime they spent quite a lot of time with them, but not so in the winter. It had been over a month since they had last seen the little monkeys and Tom and she missed them.

"Right well, Tom, maybe you could quickly vacuum the living room and sunroom and then lay the table. Don't forget Paul's coming and I think that he's bringing his girlfriend. That will be eight of us."

Tom disappeared off to get the vacuum while Rose got out the ingredients to make the spaghetti pie. She suddenly remembered that she had invited Susan to join them for lunch.

"Tom, make that nine place settings for lunch, I forgot all about Susan."

As if on cue, the telephone rang, and it was Susan herself.

"Thank goodness you've phoned. Lora never arrived in New York. Where can she be?"

"Rose, just slow down and tell me from the beginning."

Rose took a deep breath and then began again. By the time she had finished there was a silence on the other end of the line.

"Susan, are you still there?" Rose said anxiously.

"Yes, I was just thinking. You do know that I dropped her off just outside the Terminal entrance and then drove straight off.

Look, Rose, I'll be onto this straight away I just have to wind up my team meeting. I'll be around later for lunch so hopefully there will be some answers for you then."

Rose put the phone down and went back to preparing the spaghetti pie deep in thought.

Susan had stepped out of her meeting to answer Rose's call. She went back into the room where her team were chatting quietly amongst themselves.

"Right, we have another problem, Lora Du Preez has somehow disappeared. I personally dropped her off at the airport yesterday, but she never arrived at her destination which was New York. Sergeant Flowers, can you contact the airport securities and see if they have any CCTV footage from outside the terminal. Lora must have gone somewhere. She cannot have just disappeared into thin air."

"Now, back to your reports, Constable Elliot, anything on the Koreans?"

Constable Elliot stood up.

"Yes, Ma'am, it appears that one of the guests staying at The Ben Miller Inn has had his car stolen from the car park. It is a red, Corolla, license plate FMJB129.

We have put out a search warrant for it, but my guess is that our Korean friends took the car after they had dumped the Hyundai."

"Thank you, Constable. Anyone have anything else to report?"

Sergeant Mathieson stood up and pulled out his notebook.

"Yes, well, Ma'am, I interviewed a number of people in the village yesterday. As you said, it was a really good time to find a lot of people out for the town wide garage sale. Two people I spoke to," here the Sergeant referred to his notes, "Mrs. Wilson and a Ms. Coane both said that they had seen two Chinese men coming out of Renegades diner. I spoke to a couple of the waiting staff, and they confirmed that two Chinese or so they thought were Chinese, men came in for lunch on Friday at around 12:30 p.m."

Susan interjected, "Yes, and Tom Blair thought he saw a grey Hyundai parked on Colina Street on Friday at about 2:00 p.m. We know that the grey Hyundai was found on Black Point Road that evening and that a red Toyota was stolen from the Ben Miller Inn car park also that same night. We need to find that red car and soon. Is there anything else to report?"

Just then Susan's cell phone vibrated. Not another interruption, she thought as she discreetly pulled out her phone and glanced at the caller. It was the chief. She would have to take that call.

"Excuse me everyone, I'll have to take this call, it's the Chief" Susan stepped back into the lobby.

"Yes, sir, Detective Inspector Parker speaking."

"Susan, I wanted to let you know that CSIS has your girl, Lora Du Preez. They have her in a safe house here in London. I just thought that you should know. They're keeping her there apparently for her own safety."

"But why, sir, is she in any danger?"

"Well, it appears that CSIS obviously thinks that she is. Her parents were both assassinated and maybe CSIS thinks that she could be the next target. It's better this way, just leave it to CSIS. By the way, how is the investigation coming along?"

Susan had already sent him a summary of her report. She wondered if he actually ever read any of her reports.

"Yes, sir, we are making progress. We have identified the assassins although I haven't yet heard back from Interpol. They were running their mug shots through their facial recognition software to see who they are. I'll let you know as soon as we have the details. Anyway, I had better get back to my team meeting. Good day, sir."

Susan went back to the room and told the team that Lora was

in a safe house. She could see by the expressions on the men's faces that they were as puzzled as she was.

Susan was determined to get to the bottom of what was going on with CSIS. Why were they involved in the first place and what right did they have in making decisions on the safety of Lora Du Preez? What exactly did they know that she didn't?

The team meeting was concluded, and the team disbanded. It was time, Susan thought, to seek some answers from CSIS and she knew exactly where to find them.

TWENTY

"Grandma, Grandpa," Abby and Ella shrieked as the two little girls came bursting into the living room. Abby was 7 and Ella, 5, and, although they were obviously sisters, they were as different as chalk and cheese. Abby wore her dark hair tied back in a ponytail. She was a neat child, tidy in dress and appearances, whereas Ella, her little sister, had tight blonde curly hair and had a wildness about her that probably would never be tamed.

"Grandma, where's Puff and Ben?"

"Oh darlings, they're in the garden. Grandpa put them outside just because there are going to be loads of people inside."

"But Grandma, I want to see them."

Rose smiled. Abby was, if nothing else, forthright.

"Well, Abby, follow me and we'll go outside together and say hello to them."

Rose took Abby's hand and led her to the back door. Suddenly there was a shriek from Ella.

"Wait for me. I want to go, too."

Ella ran and grabbed Rose's other hand.

"Me, too, Grandma, me, too."

"Come on then you two monkeys, let's go and say hi to Ben and Puff."

Jessica was deeply engrossed in a conversation with Tom when Paul came in. He was accompanied by the most exotic looking female Tom had ever seen. She was tall, as tall as Paul himself, and had a cascade of jet-black hair which tumbled below her shoulders like a horse's mane. Her skin was a rich cinnamon and her eyes berry brown. She was stunningly beautiful.

"Dad, this is Marty, Marty, meet my father."

Marty extended a slender hand and said in a heavily accented voice.

"Pleased to meet you, sir."

"Where's Mom?" Paul asked looking around the room.

"Oh, hi there, sis," he said to Jessica. "What's up?"

Paul and Jessica didn't always see eye to eye. Growing up, it was always Jessica who would be complaining about her little brother and nothing much had changed as adults.

"Jess, this is Marty, my friend from Fanshawe College."

Jessica looked at Marty and if looks could kill poor Marty would have been dead.

Tom saw this interchange and knowing Jessica's sharp tongue, he decided to intervene quickly. "Has anyone seen your mother?"

Jessica told Tom that she had gone outside with the girls.

"Well, would anyone like a drink? Marty, Paul, Jessica, red or white wine?"

Jessica looked at her watch.

"It's a bit early to be drinking wine, dad. Shouldn't we just have coffee?"

Paul answered quickly.

"I think that I'm going to take Marty into the village. We'll grab a cup of coffee at Da Vinci's. What time will mom be serving lunch?"

Tom replied, "Oh, probably around 12ish. Have a good time and see you later."

Paul and Marty left leaving Jessica and Tom in the kitchen.

"Dad, Paul shouldn't be going out with that girl. What about Atsuko?

Tom frowned. "Well, love, your mother and I have spoken to him about that, and he says that it is all over between them. Look, it's none of our business what he does with his life."

Jessica bristled. "It is our business, Dad. I really like Atsuko and I thought mom and you did too?"

Tom looked at his feisty daughter and it suddenly dawned on him that Rob, his son-in-law was not with her.

"So, Jess, where's Rob?"

"Oh, he had some reports to write. He's up to his eyes in work right now."

"That's a shame, I was looking forward to seeing him. Is everything alright between you two?"

Jessica and Rob had experienced a hiccup in their marriage the previous year just after Paul and Atsuko's wedding, Tom thought wryly. They had patched it up and gone off on a second honeymoon to Cuba while Rose and Tom had looked after the children. Tom genuinely liked his son-in-law, Rob, and hoped that their marriage would survive. Anyone married to his daughter deserved a medal, he thought while making a pot of coffee.

Rose, Abby, and Ella, followed by two excited dogs, came charging in just as Tom was pouring out the coffee. The first thing Rose said was, "Where is Rob?" Tom explained while Jessica saw to the girls.

"Grandma, do you have any cookies?" Abby plaintively asked.

Rose looked at her watch. It was just eleven, lunch would be a good hour away, but she knew that if the girls ate too many cookies, they wouldn't eat their lunch.

"Well, dears, you may have one each because Grandma has made you your special spaghetti pie for lunch and I want you to leave room in your tummies for that."

Rose got out the cookie jar and gave Abby and Ella one each.

"Now, milk or juice to go with those cookies?"

They both chose milk and went off to the sunroom with Puff and Ben following very closely.

"So, where did Paul and his friend disappear off to?"

Jessica pulled a face and Rose could tell immediately what her daughter was thinking.

"Now, Jessica, you have to be polite to Marty even though I can tell that you do not approve. Now, where are they?"

"Oh, Mom, I liked Atsuko so much. Paul took Marty into the village. They'll be back by twelve. Can I help you with anything?"

"No, darling, just relax and enjoy your coffee, everything's under control. Oh, by the way, I invited Susan Parker to join us for lunch."

"That's great, isn't she your friend who lost her fiancé in that awful murder you were involved in last year?"

"Yes, love, her fiancé, Henri Le Bruin, was shot down at Centralia Airfield. It was so tragic. Look, don't talk about it to her - she's just about getting over it."

Jessica went quiet and then spoke softly. "I heard on the radio that there had been another couple of murders in Bayfield. Mom, please tell me that you're not involved this time?"

Rose was saved answering by Ella shrieking, "Grandma, Puff's stolen my cookie. Naughty, naughty dog."

"Don't worry, dear, come and get another one. Now, would you and Abby like to play a game with Grandma before lunch?"

"No, we want to go to the beach."

Tom had joined Rose and Jessica in the kitchen and smiled at his little forthright granddaughter.

"Well, why not, we'll all go to the beach." Turning to Rose he continued. "You can leave the pie in the oven on low, can't you, love?"

"Yes, of course, let's take advantage of this beautiful weather. Are you ready Abby? Let's get Ella and the dogs."

They were just about to leave the house when Rose remembered Susan. She would give her a call and let her know that they would be out for a walk but would be back by 12:00 p.m.

TWENTY-ONE

After Susan left the Lions Hall she drove to Da Vinci's where she picked up a coffee and then she headed straight over to Colina Street. Parking her car directly behind the big, black surveillance van, Susan got out and knocked fiercely on the driver's door. The window was lowered and a pleasant looking man wearing headphones answered.

"Oh, how can I help you, ma'am?"

Susan could see another man sitting at the rear of the van. His face was lit up presumably by some sort of screen monitor. Susan tried to see more but, short of cramming her head through the window, it was impossible to make out all the equipment she assumed was installed in the van.

She replied at the same time as pulling out her warrant card.

"I am Detective Inspector Parker and I have reason to believe that you had the property belonging to Rose and Tom Blair on Bayfield Terrace under surveillance? Your drone has been hovering over their house for the past three days. You do know that it is illegal to be spying on anyone."

The pleasant faced young man pulled out his warrant card.

"Agent Roberts at your service, Ma'am. I work for CSIS, and we are under official orders to watch the Blairs."

Susan bristled before saying, "I demand to speak to your senior officer. I have many questions to ask him, one of them being why should the Blairs be under surveillance in the first place? Could you please put me in contact with your Chief?"

Susan had used her most authoritative voice and hoped it would do the trick.

Agent Roberts spoke through his microphone attached to his bulletproof vest, "This is Agent Roberts here. Yes, I have a Detective Parker wanting to speak to you, sir."

He listened carefully to the reply and then turned to Susan. "The Chief will meet with you tomorrow at eleven o'clock here in this van."

"Thank you, Agent, I'll see you tomorrow."

Finally, Susan thought, *I might get some answers.*

She drove around the corner to Rose and Tom's house on Bayfield Terrace and was just pulling into the drive when Paul and Marty came walking up the road, hand in hand. Susan jumped out of the car and walked over to greet them.

"How are you doing?"

Paul gave Susan a quick hug.

"Susan, this is Marty, she's at Fanshawe College."

"Hi, Marty, are you a lecturer or a student, I can never tell the difference these days?"

Marty smiled: her beautiful pearly white teeth shone out against her dusky skin.

"I learn economics," she said with her thick accent, "Paul, he teach me English."

"Where are you from, Marty?" Susan asked wondering where this beautiful exotic girl had come from.

Paul chipped in, "She's from Spain. Pamplona. That's northern Spain, near the Pyrenees."

Susan smiled. "I know where Pamplona is, the running of the bulls. I've always wanted to visit that part of Spain. It's Basque country, isn't it?"

'Yes, we are very proud to be Basque people."

"Paul, I've been invited to lunch. Are your parents in? Were you about to go inside?"

"We've just come back from the village. I assume Mom and Dad are inside."

They had walked up to the front door and Paul opened it calling out, "Mom, Dad, Susan's here."

There was no answer.

"Maybe they're all in the garden?" Paul said walking to the back door. He popped his head outside and returned seconds later.

"Nope, not there. My guess is they've taken Puff and Ben and those monkeys Abby and Ella down to the beach. Never mind, they'll be back soon. Can I get you something to drink, Susan? Come and sit in the sunroom and I'll bring us all out a drink."

So, Susan thought, *Rose and Tom have done it again, gone out without locking up the house. Just wait until they come back,* she thought, *I'll give them what for then.*

Lora paced up and down like a caged animal. It was bad enough not being able to leave the house, but what was even worse was having her cell phone taken away. She was unable to phone Celia to reassure her that she was okay, and she could only imagine how worried her friend would be not knowing where on earth she had gone to.

Nobody spoke to her. The fridge had been stocked up with food, so she was able to make herself some simple meals. There was a television that she could watch and also an Apple box which enabled her to watch Netflix. There was, however, a limit to how many movies she could watch or, indeed, want to watch in a day. How much longer would she remain incarcerated in that house Lora did not know, but one thing she knew for certain was that she would go stark crazy mad if left alone much longer.

Abby, Ella, and the dogs had burst through the front door and, before Susan could think about admonishing Tom and Rose, they followed the children along with Jessica all laughing and in such good spirits it would have been a shame to have broken the mood.

"Oh, we're so sorry to be late. I see that Paul let you in. Right, lunch will be ready in about twenty minutes. Susan, could I have a quick word with you."

Susan got up and followed Rose into the kitchen.

"Is there any news about Lora? I cannot stop thinking about her."

"Well, actually I know where she is, although I still haven't got to the bottom of it. CSIS have her in a safe house somewhere in London. They fear for her safety. That's all I know."

Rose looked so relieved yet also puzzled. "A safe house, but why?"

She paused before saying, "Oh well, at least she's safe. Can I let her friend Celia know that she's okay?"

"Yes, and maybe she can let her bosses at the UN know that she's helping us with our enquiries. Now, let's forget about this for the time being and enjoy our lunch. Abby, Ella, come and talk to your Aunty Susan."

The girls loved Susan. They squealed with delight when she grabbed their hands and started dancing around the room with them.

Rose threw an apron on and began to chop kale, tomatoes, and cucumber to make a healthy salad to accompany the not so healthy spaghetti pie.

The rest of the day whizzed by with all the laughter and talk that families make when together. Soon, though, Paul and Marty made their excuses and left, followed shortly by Jessica and two tired and protesting, little girls. Susan was the last to leave. She thanked Rose and Tom profusely.

'Thank you, dear friend. I just love getting together with all your family. Well, not quite all. How is Anne getting on and how is that adorable baby, Oliver?"

Anne, Rose and Tom's youngest daughter, lived in Halifax with her professor husband, Alan, and their precious fourteen-month-old baby, Oliver. Tom and Rose had been out to visit them just before going off on their safari. Anne had just recently returned to work at Dalhousie University having finished her maternity leave. She was still adjusting to the hectic and exhausting life of a working mom, although Alan was proving to be an excellent father. Two days a week he looked after Oliver, the other three, the baby went to the university Day Care and then either Anne or Alan would drop off or pick him up according to their lecture schedules.

They seemed to be coping alright, although the other night when Rose had spoken to Anne, she had sounded very tired and quite weepy. Maybe it was time she and Tom flew out for another visit, Rose thought as she hugged her friend Susan and bade her farewell.

The house was blissfully quiet after everyone had left. Tom made a pot of tea and carried it through to the sunroom where Rose had her feet up on the sofa.

They were just drinking their tea when there was a loud knock on their front door. Puff and Ben barked and ran to the door followed closely by Tom. Two men in dark suits stood on the doorstep. Rose got up and walked over to see what they wanted. It wouldn't be the Jehovah's Witnesses as they never came calling on a Sunday. The taller of the two men stepped forward and pulled out a Warrant card.

"Agent Roberts. We're here to detain you and your wife."

Tom and Rose looked bewildered and shocked. Tom said in a shaky voice.

"Did you say detain as in taking us away or keeping us here? What do you mean?"

Rose stood next to Tom and looked at both men. They did look rather formidable, yet they had been very polite.

"You need to come with us. We have a few questions to ask you both."

"What about our dogs? How long will we be?" Rose said now feeling distinctly nervous at the prospect of leaving the house with the strange men.

"You will be back before long. Your dogs will be fine, ma'am."

"Well, at least give me time to feed them before we go."

Rose picked up Ben and Puff's dog bowls and went to the pantry to get their Kibbles. Getting out her iPhone which Rose now carried everywhere, she sent Susan a text message, *CSIS have taken us for questioning.*

Pouring the kibbles into the dogs' dishes Rose returned carrying the bowls and put them on the floor.

"Right, are you ready, Mrs. Blair?"

"Yes, I'm coming."

Tom and Rose were ushered out to a black sedan. Agent Roberts opened the back passenger door and the Blairs got in. Rose gave Tom a scared look. She did not want to get into any confrontation with these men.

They drove off at high speed towards London.

TWENTY-TWO

Susan got back to her condo still smiling. She had experienced such a good time and Rose and Tom had truly made her feel part of the family.

She looked at her watch, it was almost 5:00 p.m. and Peter Joyce would be arriving quite soon. They hadn't even talked about dinner and if Susan was truthful, she really wasn't after food, well, not that sort of food, besides, she was still full from the huge lunch at Rose and Tom's.

She opened her fridge to see what there was inside. Nothing but a few mouldy carrots, some cheese and an old shriveled up lettuce. Well, that made the decision easy, she thought as she brushed her hair and applied some lipstick. They would go out for dinner, and she would let Peter choose which restaurant.

Susan had just about finished tidying up the living room when there was a knock on the door. It was Peter. He entered carrying a bottle of wine and a beautiful bunch of roses.

Susan took the wine and the flowers and then wrapped her arms around his neck.

"Peter, thank you darling," and they began to kiss a slow, deep, and passionate kiss. Before they could stop each other, Susan was pulling at Peter's shirt buttons, and he was lifting her dress over her head and then they were on the sofa in the living room. Their love making was fierce and urgent and left them both panting and replete. Peter laughed as he untwined his legs and looked down upon Susan's body.

"Have I even said hallo to you Susie? Have I told you that I missed you? I want to devour every inch of your sexy body."

Susan laughed and sat up suddenly aware of the fact that the curtains were wide open, and it was still daylight. Fortunately, the condos were private, and she rarely saw anyone outside, but lying there completely stark naked made her feel a bit embarrassed. Susan got up and padded into the hallway picking up the trail of clothing that had been thrown off their bodies in the height of their passion.

She glanced at herself in the hall mirror and saw that her face was flushed pink, and her lips bruised red. Her hair was tussled everywhere. She truly looked as if she had been ravaged in bed. Peter joined her and wrapped his arms around her, nuzzling her neck.

"Peter, we're going out for dinner. Where do you fancy?"

Twenty minutes later Susan and Peter sat at a table for two in Our Thai, a red candle flickering on the table and a gentle jazz number playing in the background. They had just placed their orders when Susan's phone vibrated. She had set it to vibrate so as not to disturb the diners.

"Excuse, me Peter," Susan said as she checked the text message that had come in. It was from Rose and as she read the short message her heart made a lurch. What on earth were CSIS playing at now?

Peter could see that the mood had been broken by that single call Susan had just received.

"Is everything alright darling?"

Susan let out a deep sigh.

"No, Peter, my work is never done and this time I'm up against a greater power and I don't know exactly how to deal with them. I have the Canadian Security Intelligence Service on my case, and I don't even know why."

"You mean CSIS? Wow, they are the equivalent of the CIA. What on earth would they be doing in Bayfield? Is it connected to those two murders?"

"Yes, but I can't really talk about it. I'm just not sure how to handle them. I know that CSIS has a mandate to collect and analyse intelligence both domestic and international, but as far as I'm concerned that does not mean they could or should be interfering with any local police investigations. Now, my friends, Rose and Tom, have been hauled in for questioning and I feel that my hands have been tied."

Peter took one of Susan's hands and kissed it.

"Well, it sounds as if there is nothing that you can do about it tonight so you might as well enjoy this meal and hopefully by tomorrow all will be sorted out. I'm sure that your friends will be treated with all due respect so don't worry."

"Yes, I know that you're right, Peter. Now, this Pad Thai looks delicious and so does your green curry. Can I try a spoonful of yours?"

TWENTY-THREE

Rose and Tom were driven to the safe house in London. When Lora saw them, she burst into tears.

"Oh, Rose and Tom, I've been so worried. I've felt like a prisoner. Have you come to take me home?"

Tom shook his head and explained that they too had been dragged in for questioning.

"But why? What do they think you've done? Surely they don't think you had anything to do with Mom and Dad's death, do they?" Lora said looking really confused.

Rose answered her quietly, "Well, our house has been under surveillance all week, well, since the first murder." Rose stopped and squeezed Lora's arm before continuing, "Sorry, Lora, I shouldn't have mentioned it but somehow since your parents' death we have been put on their list of suspects."

Tom interrupted Rose, "I've been thinking about that, love, and I suppose I can understand in a way why they should be suspicious. We did meet up with Lora's parents in Kenya and then they were coming to visit us here in Bayfield. If nothing else we are guilty by association. I can only think that the CSIS are involved because the Du Preez's are from overseas. What do you think, Lora?"

Tom never heard what Lora had to say because the front door was opened and a big, burly man dressed once again in a black suit, appeared. He held in his hand a clip board and he looked all business and very officious.

"Rose Blair, come this way, please."

Rose paled and she clutched Tom's hand.

"I'll come with you," Tom said, but the man firmly replied.

"No, we want to talk to you both separately. Now come along, Rose, let's get this over and done with as I'm sure that you want to get home to those dogs of yours."

At the mention of Puff and Ben, Rose stiffened and let go of Tom's hand.

"Alright, let's get it over with."

Rose was led into another room which had padded walls. There was a single small table with two ladder backed chairs facing each other. It all reminded Rose of some of the old spy movies that she had watched as a teenager. They had been in black and white; *Thirty-Nine Steps* came to mind. But this certainly was no movie set and it was in full blown technicolour.

She sat down on one of the chairs and looked closely at the man now seated opposite her. He was in his mid-fifties, she guessed, with grey hair, receding at the forehead, he had a florid complexion and a hard, square jaw line that immediately made Rose feel frightened.

"Your name is Rose Blair, I am correct?"

Rose nodded.

"This interview is being recorded; you need to answer me fully."

'Yes, my name is Rose Blair."

"What is your connection to the deceased?"

"Tom and I met Andre and Jan when we went on a safari in Kenya this past March. We knew them for all of ten days. I was surprised when we received a post card from New York saying that they were coming to visit us in Bayfield. That was the last that we heard from them."

The agent went quiet and peered at Rose with his rheumy eyes.

'Are you quite sure that was the last you heard from them?"

Rose gulped. Why was it that she was made to feel like a criminal?

"Well, there was a phone call from Andre wanting to talk to Tom, but I swear that is the last connection that we had after the safari."

"Well, why is it that we have CCTV footage taken on the same day that Jan was murdered showed Andre Du Preez walking into your house? He was there for a good twenty minutes. He even let your dogs into the back yard and then let himself out ten minutes later. How can you account for that? Where were you at the time?"

At least the mystery of the break in had been solved, Rose thought whilst trying to process what the agent was implying.

"I was down at the docks, having discovered Jan's body floating in the water, and Tom was out playing golf. It was a complete and baffling mystery to both of us as to why the dogs were outside when we had clearly left them inside. So, how did you know that Andre had entered our house?" As the words were out of her mouth, Rose immediately knew the answer to her own question. It was the crow drone. *Just what else had the drone recorded,* she wondered and then thought about the stolen slip of paper.

"You obviously do not believe in locking your front door, Mrs. Blair. We have footage showing a red Toyota pulling up outside your house just after you, your husband and Lora Du Preez went out with the dogs. Two men, Koreans, got out and entered your house, retreating twenty minutes later. Now my question to you is, what was Andre Du Preez looking for in your house? It is just too much of a coincidence that the Du Preez's had their own house in Windhoek broken in to and just freshly received from Interpol, Lora Du Preez has also had her apartment in New York burgled. What are they looking for?"

Rose suddenly felt angry. What right had they, CSIS, to be treating Tom and her like common criminals when they had done nothing. She felt her face going red. Rose took a deep breath and willed herself to reign in her rising temper.

"If we knew what they were looking for we would have told Detective Parker. We are not hiding anything."

Suddenly Rose realized that what she had just said was actually untrue. Tom and she were actually hiding the coded number sheets. Surely they couldn't be that important? Should she come clean, Rose thought, or not? In the end Rose decided that they would hand the deciphered sheets of paper over to Susan and not to the bully CSIS Agent.

After they finished interrogating Rose the CSIS Agent called Tom into the room and proceeded to grill him as he had with Rose. Finally, at about nine o'clock that night, Agent Roberts appeared and took Rose and Tom back to the car. They bid a teary farewell to Lora and promised to be in touch just as soon as she was released. Rose also said that she would speak to Lora's friend Celia and assure her that Lora was okay.

TWENTY-FOUR

Peter and Susan stayed up late talking. Over a couple of bottles of wine Susan learnt just a little more about the man she felt that she was falling quite deeply in love with. He was very private and it was rather like piecing together a jigsaw with the fragments of information that he dropped into their conversation.

She could tell that he had been deeply hurt by someone and that he had been in a relationship with that person for over ten years. It had been a case of once bitten twice shy.

After the split up he had thrown himself into his work, taking every assignment offered until one day he woke up and said enough was enough. His life afterwards had slowed down and had become more stable, so much so that he could step back and smell the roses and dream about retirement.

Susan yawned and sleepily said,

'My darling, I would love you to spend the night, but I have an early team meeting and I need to get my sleep. When can we meet again?"

Peter looked deeply into Susan's eyes.

"We'll have to slow down a bit you know, I'm falling head over heels in love with you and it feels almost out of control. I want to spend every waking hour of the day with you but yes, we both still have work to do. What about Wednesday, I can come here, or you could come to London?"

Susan thought, she wanted to meet with the Chief, but wasn't sure if he would be free on Wednesday or not.

"I'll find out my schedule, Peter, and let you know. If I must be in London anyway on Wednesday it would make sense for me to come to you. I'll let you know tomorrow."

They kissed deeply and then Peter left leaving Susan feeling sleepily content and wondering if she too was falling head over heels in love with the enigmatic photographer.

Rose and Tom didn't get to bed that night until well past midnight. Neither of them could sleep; they both felt over-whelmed by that evening's events. They had been dropped off outside their house at ten o'clock and had been greeted by two very anxious dogs. Tom immediately grabbed their leashes and told Rose he would take them for a quick walk around the block.

His ulterior motive was to check to see if the black van was still parked on Colina Street. Tom had just left the house when the telephone rang. It was Jessica, a decidedly annoyed Jessica.

"Mom, have you looked at Facebook? You and dad are plas-tered all over it. Those people murdered in Bayfield were friends of yours?"

Rose interrupted their daughter. "What do you mean on Facebook?"

"Check it out, Mom, there's a picture of you and dad down by *Tranquility*. It looks like an old photo because your hair is shorter, anyway, the headlines run, *Another Murder in Bayfield*. Honestly, Mom, you promised not to get involved ever again and look at this, both you and Dad."

'Now, hold on, Jessica," Rose said, "It's not our fault that our friends got murdered. Instead of being so indignant you might think about how upsetting it's been for us. Now, I really am very tired, I need to go to bed. Good night."

Normally Rose wouldn't have been so curt with her daughter, but the evening that they had just spent being grilled by CSIS had well and truly tried her nerves. I am too old for all of this, Rose thought. Putting the phone down she noticed the flashing message light. She pressed the retrieve button and listened.

It was Jean from the Croquet Club wondering why Tom and Rose had not attended the opening of the season cocktail party at the Town Hall and were they both okay?

Tom and she had completely forgotten about the cocktail party with everything going on and they were supposed to be bringing Susan along as a potential new member too. *Oh well,* Rose thought, *we'll go out and play the following Thursday and maybe invite Susan to join us then.*

There were four other messages all enquiring about the Facebook postings. Rose got out her tablet and opened the Facebook page. Jessica was right, there were at least half a dozen postings all pretty well saying the same thing. Absolutely nothing could be secret anymore, social media was just all pervasive.

Tom returned with Puff and Ben and said, "It's still there, the black van."

"Well, did you think that it would magically disappear, Tom. It will be there until they've caught the murderer." Rose said still feeling snappy after her telephone call from Jessica. "Look, Tom, look at all these Facebook postings."

Tom scrolled through and raised his eyebrows.

"Well, we're infamous now, love."

Rose made them both some hot chocolate which they took to bed. They were both still too wired up for sleep.

"Did you mention anything about the pieces of paper with the coded numbers, Tom?" Rose asked while changing into her nightie.

"No, I didn't, but I reckon that we need to pass them onto Susan, either that or lock them up in a safe box in the bank. It's obvious that they're hot potatoes. What do you reckon, love, the bank or Susan?"

"Well, I'd really like to know what it all means. I was going to look at the map tomorrow and see if I could find some co-ordinates that match what I have written down. After that, we can hand them over to Susan."

"I suppose another day won't make any difference. Right now, I'm going to try to forget about everything and get some sleep. Night, night, love." Tom turned off his bedside lamp and Rose sat for a while in complete darkness before she too lay down and closed her eyes although sleep completely evaded her.

TWENTY-FIVE

The team was all assembled and raring to go in the Lions Hall. Susan had woken up feeling somewhat hung over after all the wine that she had consumed with Peter the night before. She arrived at the meeting five minutes later than her team.

"Good morning, everyone. I hope that you all had a good weekend such time that you managed to grab with your families between meetings. Now, we are into Day 6 of our investigation, and we need to get some results as this case is beginning to drag and lose momentum. Right, reports, please. Sergeant Mathieson."

The Sergeant stood up, "Not much to report, Ma'am, other than a sighting in Lambton County of a red Toyota Corolla driven by two Asian men around 3:00 p.m. yesterday just outside Port Franks on Highway 21. That's all, Ma'am."

Susan had opened her laptop and was scrolling through her emails when she paused and read intently a report sent to her from Interpol. She looked up from her computer and said, "Sorry, Sergeant, I did hear your report, but I've just received some key information from Interpol. They have the results back from the facial recognition software. Our two Koreans are, Kim Jejoon and Lee Simm. They are from Pyong Yang, the capital of North Korea, however, Interpol says that the two men have been living in Namibia on and off these past few years. Now, listen to this, both men are known assassins. Their names have come up blocked in red for dangerous. They have been linked with corporate killings throughout the world and so far, have eluded the authorities. Men, we are dealing with extremely ruthless killers.

Now, Lora Du Preez has been tracked down to a safe house in London and is fine. Her life could be at stake, and she will be kept at the safe house until the assassins have been caught. I have also to report that the Blair's," Susan looked pointedly over at Mathieson, "were taken in for questioning last night by CSIS. They were released and driven back home. I will be meeting with them later on this morning. I also have a meeting with an agent from CSIS. Their involvement makes me nervous, and I need to get Constable some answers from them before we can proceed with our enquiry. We still are no closer to finding the motive for these killings. It has to be of international importance to have CSIS involved, but what it is has eluded this case from the beginning."

"Sergeant Mathieson, I would like you to get back to researching what it was that the Du Preez's worked on in Namibia. They were obviously wealthy judging by the huge house they lived in. Look into everything and anything unusual happening in Windhoek over the past two years. If this is an international crime, we need to cast our nets further and look at this more on a global scale. Constables Elliot and Brown, keep up the interviewing of local people. My guess is we haven't seen the last of the Koreans. If they haven't yet found what they're looking for then they definitely will be back. I would also like a watch put on the Blair's home. Sergeant Flowers could you arrange that? My instinct tells me that they will be the next targets purely by their association with the Du Preez's."

"Right, I want results and soon. Let's meet again at the same time tomorrow."

The meeting disbanded and Susan typed up her daily report. She then put a call into London requesting to speak to the Chief. She was put through to his secretary who checked his diary to see if he was available for a meeting that Wednesday. His calendar was open, so Susan booked an afternoon meeting with him. She would go straight from that meeting to Peter's house. With that all settled, Susan tidied up her workplace and quietly left the Lions Hall.

TWENTY-SIX

Rose and Tom slept in late, and both woke up bleary eyed.

"Was that all one horrible nightmare last night, love?" Tom sleepily murmured to Rose.

"Gosh, I wish it was, but no, we were actually interrogated like criminals, and I still feel really angry about it," Rose retorted now fully awake.

"Calm down, love, no harm's been done, CSIS are just doing their job."

"Well, they shouldn't waste their time and energy on innocent people like us. They should be chasing the murderers, not us."

"Interesting, though, about Andre snooping around our house and then those Koreans doing the same thing. Didn't Susan say they were chasing two Asian men in a grey car? I reckon they're the assassins, but heaven knows why Andre and Jan should be murdered."

"Tom, shouldn't you be playing golf with Doug this morning?"

Rose looked at her watch. It was almost nine o'clock. Tom jumped out of bed saying "Yes, he'll be here any minute now."

"I'll go and make some tea and put on some toast while you get dressed. Doug won't mind waiting a few minutes while you eat your breakfast."

Rose put on her dressing gown and padded to the kitchen. She let Ben and Puff outside and then put the kettle on for tea. She was just reaching for the bread when her phone rang. It was Jean from the Croquet Club.

"I've been reading all about you and Tom on Facebook. We knew about the murders but didn't know that you were actually involved. But that's not why I'm calling. Would you and Tom like to join us for a game of croquet tomorrow morning"

Rose thought for a minute.

"Yes, why not, it's about time that we put those mallets to use again. What time, Jean?"

"About eleven would be good. It will give some time for the sun to dry the dew out of the grass."

"Okay, I look forward to it. See you and Mike tomorrow."

Mike, Jean's husband, was a retired lawyer from Brampton. They had moved to the village ten years ago and lived on Tuyl Street. Rose liked them very much and so did Tom.

Thinking about croquet, Rose remembered inviting Susan to the cocktail party. Maybe, if she was free the next day, she could accompany them to the courts and have a little practice.

Doug arrived just as Tom sat down to eat his toast. Rose invited Doug in and offered him a cup of tea.

'No, thank you, Rose, I'm a coffee man."

"I can make you a coffee if you want?" Rose said, but Doug declined. She could see that he was anxious to get out onto the golf course.

"I could put your tea in a cup to go, Tom," she said hoping that Tom would take the hint and speed up eating his breakfast.

Finally, Tom rose, gulped the last bit of tea, gave Rose a kiss on her cheek, and off the two men went for a morning of golf. Rose had the kitchen to herself again, well, almost to herself as she shared it with her two constant companions, Puff and Ben.

She received four phone calls from different friends all enquiring about the murder. Everyone had read the details on Facebook, but now they wanted the dirt from Rose herself. *Blasted social media*, Rose thought as she explained for the fourth time how Tom and she barely knew the Du Preez's. Talking about them made Rose remember her promise to Lora that she would contact her friend Celia and let her know that she was alright.

Tapping Celia's cell number in Rose was amazed how fast it was picked up.

"Celia," Rose said, "I have some good news for you. Lora is fine. She's in a safe house, she just wanted you to know that she's fine, but could you please notify her boss that she will be back at work soon."

Celia exclaimed, "But why is she in a safe house? Oh, and by the way, our apartment was broken into a couple of nights ago. I was visiting my family at the time, but when I returned, I found the front door open, and Lora's computer had been stolen. Nothing else was taken which is really weird, particularly for New York."

It gets stranger, Rose thought.

"Well, thank goodness you were out, Celia. There are a lot of very strange things happening at the moment and it's all to do with something the Du Preez's have, and some Koreans want to retrieve it. It's very puzzling, but CSIS are on to it. They're a bit like your CIA or FBI, not sure which one?"

"You probably mean Homeland Security, but whatever, it's obviously an international threat of some kind."

Rose continued to talk to Celia a while longer and then ended the conversation. She went back to the kitchen to start on the cleanup. The house looked a tip from the previous day. With all that had happened neither Rose nor Tom had time to unload the dishwasher or clean the pots and pans piled up in the sink. The living room needed vacuuming too. Whenever the dogs came back from the beach, sand was found everywhere and if one went bare-foot, it was very gritty. Rose got busy doing the housework.

Halfway through vacuuming, the telephone rang again. It was Lena.

"Rose, I sold everything including all those suitcases. Two Asian looking men bought the whole lot of them. I made over $300. Anyway, thanks a bunch for donating your stuff. Can I pay you some of the money?"

"Oh, Lena, no, of course not. You did us a favour taking all of it off our hands. But you could take me out for a cup of coffee. I'm looking for an excuse to get out of doing this very boring housework."

Lena laughed, "How about eleven. It's ten o'clock now, that will give you time to finish off what you're doing. See you later."

Rose went back to the housework with a smile on her face. At least she only had one hour left.

Just as Rose was preparing to walk into the village to meet Lena for coffee, Susan was getting ready to meet up with the CSIS agent at the black van parked on Colina Street. She drove and parked her car behind the van. Knocking on the driver's door, Susan jumped when the side door swung open, and a good-looking man climbed out.

Susan gauged him to be in his forties with a look of Brad Pitt about him. He had sandy blond hair, piercing blue eyes and a disarming smile. Of course, he was wearing what looked like the statutory issue black suit. Susan could see that under the jacket he wore a pistol tucked into a black leather holster. She, too, carried a gun, mostly tucked into her pants at the back.

He extended his hand to Susan.

"Hi. I'm Agent Lewis. I presume that you are Detective Susan Parker?"

"Yes. I have a few urgent questions to ask you. Can we go somewhere to talk?"

Agent Lewis beckoned for Susan to follow him into the van. The back of the van was all about technology with television screens everywhere and on each screen, Susan could see the Blair's house - front, back, and sides.

There was a car seat in the middle and Agent Lewis sidled in next to Susan.

"Fire away, Detective, I have about 30 minutes to give you before lunch and then I'm on the road again. What is it that you want to know?"

He smiled once again in his very disarming manner. It fairly took the wind out of Susan's sail. She arrived ready to make war with CSIS, but she had not reckoned on Agent Lewis's charm.

"Well, what I really want to know is why do you have the Blair's under surveillance?" she pointed to the screens, "It seems way over the top and such a waste of your resources to be watching them as if they are the prime suspects in this murder case."

Agent Lewis kept quiet and so Susan continued, "And another thing, why haul Lora Du Preez off to a safe house? Surely you cannot believe that her life could be in danger?"

The Agent still kept his silence. Susan recklessly continued, "You do realize that I am conducting this double murder enquiry and I personally view your involvement as obstructive and unnecessary."

Susan stopped and waited for some reaction from Agent Lewis. He finally bent forward and pulled out a dossier that had been sitting on the central console of the van. Opening the file, he removed two sheets of paper and passed them over to Susan to read. Each paper had a photograph clipped to the top. These were the files on the two Koreans.

Susan scanned the papers quickly, much of this she had already read from the Interpol report. She knew that they were trained assassins but had not realized that they were professional mercenaries open to contracts from all over the world. They had been living in Windhoek the past few months, presumably watching the Du Preez's and waiting for instructions.

The list of homicides related to the Koreans was extensive. Some of the names were familiar to Susan, many were not, but one thing that came over loud and clear was that these men had eluded capture for over ten years. They were good and very dangerous.

Agent Lewis started to talk, "You ask why the daughter is in a safe house? Well, in the past, these assassins have murdered whole families. We cannot take that risk with Lora. Judging from the break-ins, it appears that these men are seriously looking for something. Now, there has to be more than these two assassins involved as Lora's apartment was broken into in New York while the Koreans were still around here."

Susan interrupted him.

"Yes, they were spotted in Lambton County just two days ago when Lora's place was burgled so they couldn't have been in New York then."

Agent Lewis continued, "I need to warn you, Detective that we have been watching these men for years. They are extremely dangerous. Now, you ask why CSIS has been involved in this murder case and I have told you about our interest in the Koreans, but our biggest draw was the deceased couple, Andre and Jan Du Preez. What I tell you here will go no further, do you understand?"

Susan blanched and nodded her head.

"Your murdered couple were recruits of Mossad, the Israeli spy agency. That is why CSIS is involved."

Susan looked incredulous.

"Are you sure? I can't believe that they were actual spies. Why?"

Agent Lewis pulled out another dossier and another sheet of paper. He handed it over to Susan to read.

Apparently Andre and Jan Du Preez had been recruited by Mossad when they were young graduates working on the Kibutz in Israel. They had been active Mossad agents for over thirty years and were high-ranking code breakers.

"Wow," Susan said as she handed back the sheet of paper to Agent Lewis, "So that still begs the question, why?"

Agent Lewis smiled, "Yes, that million-dollar question, what is the motive? Well, as you can imagine we have our own spies all over the world. Namibia has been on our radar for a few years now. Do you know that Namibia is tremendously rich in natural resources? There are three international mining corporations all based in that country and I know that you will be familiar with the De Beers Diamonds, but what is lesser known are the base metals mined in that country. There are huge mining conglomerates with gold, silver, and a very large uranium mine owned by a British company. Now, MI6 in England have been watching the uranium mining business very closely. Earlier this year we received a report from our own CSIS agent based in Windhoek. The report listed unusual covert activity on the mine."

Susan interrupted Agent Lewis once more,

"Where in Namibia is this uranium mining facility?"

"It's almost 100km north of Windhoek, just off the Namib Highway, south of the Caprivi Strip.

"But there are uranium mines all over the world, what's so

special about this facility?" Susan said still trying to work out where all the information was going.

"Do you have any knowledge on how nuclear weapons are developed?"

Susan bristled. Agent Lewis was beginning to irritate her with his condescending attitude.

"Yes, well, no, I know that the uranium has to be enriched but that's about as far as my knowledge goes."

"Well, I'm not about to lecture you now. Needless to say, it's a complicated process. Enrichment involves the removal of U238. We believe that the Koreans have developed a laser enrichment processing plant and here lies the real global threat. Our sources in southwest Africa, combined with the MI6 reports, all suggest to us that North Korea might be making weapons of mass destruction somewhere in the Namib Desert."

"Well, "Susan said, "surely that would be easy to spot. You can't tell me that the whole area hasn't been searched and surveyed by now?"

"Yes, we have scoured every inch of the desert, but cannot see any sign of an enrichment plant. We think that it is probably located underground."

"But how does this all tie in with Andre and Jan Du Preez?"

"What we think is that Israel also got onto the fact that the Koreans were making nuclear weapons and, as Andre and Jan were already seasoned operative Mossad agents, plus the fact that they lived in the area, they would have been put on a fact-finding mission. It could be that they discovered the location of the uranium enrichment plant and maybe that is why they have been killed. We don't know, but that could be one explanation."

Agent Lewis looked at his watch.

"Look, can I call you Susan?"

Susan nodded, "Yes, of course but only if you let me know your first name. I can't keep calling you Agent Lewis?"

He smiled and said, "Actually, my name is Andrew, but you can call me Andy. But Susan, it is lunch time now and I'm starving hungry, would you care to join me for lunch at The Little Inn?"

Susan looked at her watch and sure enough it was gone 12:00. *Lunch would be just great,* she thought as she noticed that Andrew Lewis drove a silver Porsche Carrera. *He was definitely a player,* she thought as she followed him in her car and parked outside of The Little Inn.

"Do you want to eat in The tap room or the main restaurant, Andy?" Susan asked.

The Little Inn had changed hands and now sported two eating areas. Andrew looked at the menu posted outside next to the entry to the Inn.

"Definitely the main restaurant for me. I see that mussels are on the menu."

Susan really hated mussels, but she knew that there was a good and varied choice of entrees to choose from the menu.

Over the following hour Agent Lewis and Susan discussed everything but the case. She found Andrew good company as he was both sharp and witty too.

"So, where do you live, Andrew?"

"Well, CSIS is based in Ottawa. I live in Gatineau Park just across the river and before you ask, I am married and have two teenage children and one dog. I also have looked at your dossier and I know all about your dreadful loss. I saw that you had retired from the police force. How come you're still investigating murders?"

Susan was quite shocked to hear that Andrew had read up all about her life. But CSIS was a spy agency so what did she really expect, she thought wryly. At least the man was honest and that in itself was quite refreshing.

"I was asked if I would come back to investigate the murder of Andre Du Preez because, firstly, I live here in Bayfield and secondly, they are short staffed at the Serious Crimes Division in London. I've also worked with my team before, and we have a good working relationship."

"Um... your team. I shouldn't really be telling you this, Susan, but you do have a mole in your works. No, I exaggerate, he's not really a 'mole', more of a snitch, but just watch your back. One of your 'team' has been passing on information to us, I think that he has aspirations to join the CSIS team. I won't tell you who it is, but just be warned."

"My Chief in Headquarters had warned me as well, I have a fair idea who the squealer is, but I have no proof. Thank you for letting me know, I appreciate it."

They continued eating their delicious lunch in pleasant harmony, oblivious to the fact that cruising down Main Street, in a white Ford Focus recently stolen in Grand Bend, the two Koreans were planning their next move.

TWENTY-SEVEN

L ena and Rose enjoyed a coffee together at Da Vinci's. Both women sat on the Town Hall committee and the Historical Society board, and they often talked about issues concerning the two committees. The next big fundraiser for the Town Hall was the chicken barbeque called 'Sunset on Summer,' and that wasn't until Labour Day weekend. Before that there were a few concert events, but mostly in the summer months the Town Hall was used primarily for weddings.

"So, Rose, I saw you and Tom plastered all over Facebook. I bet you're not too happy about that. Who do you think posted it all?"

Rose pulled a face. "You know, Lena, I haven't a clue. I've wondered about that."

"Well, I'm sure they didn't mean to be malicious or anything, but it might have been nice if they'd asked you first."

"Oh, well, it's yesterday's news, there will be another story today to occupy the voyeurs. So, Lena, tell me all about the book you're working on for the Historical Society."

Lena spent the following ten minutes telling Rose all about the story on Admiral Bayfield she was writing. She had done a fair bit of research and was excited that Bob, her husband, and she, were going to Charlottetown on Prince Edward Island where Admiral Bayfield had spent his retirement.

"And we're going to see where he lived and where the Admiralty was based. I can hardly wait."

"When do you leave, Lena?" Rose enquired.

"Next week. We're flying to Halifax and then renting a car. By the way, Rose, do you want me to take anything out for Anne? We could easily manage to meet up with her."

"Oh, Lena, that would be fantastic. I spoke to Anne the other day and she sounded a bit down. She's back working again, and I think that being a working mom is getting her down. I'll put together some small gifts for them and if you could deliver the package not only will Anne be delighted to see you, but you can report back to me how she is really coping. Tom and I might visit them maybe next month, we'll have to see."

The two women finished their coffee and then left Da Vinci's café. Rose walked up to Charles Street and turned right towards Louisa Street. She passed where Maud Stirling and her sister had lived out their retirement. Maud had been a nursing sister in the First World War. She had been sent out to Salonika, Greece to a thousand-bed tented hospital. The conditions were horrific with bombs dropping and fleas, rats, and lice everywhere. The nurses not only had to contend with bombs dropping from the sky, but the permanent itching of crawling lice. Kerosene was used to wash the nurse's hair in an attempt to get rid of the lice. Maud was awarded the Royal Red Cross Award for Bravery.

As Rose walked along Louisa Street past where the mayor lived, she became aware of a white car driving slowly behind her. She looked over her shoulder and to her absolute horror she realized that she was staring right into the faces of the two Korean men Susan had told Tom and her about.

Rose walked faster and faster and turned onto Bayfield Terrace. She could see their neighbour, Greg, in his front garden trimming the hedge. Walking up to him quickly she started to engage him in conversation.

"Beautiful day, Greg, isn't it?"

"Sure is, Rose, sure is. Where's that husband of yours? Out playing golf again, is he?"

"Yes, I'm truly a golf widow, Greg. How's Eileen?"

Eileen had been very sick following a trip to Peru. She had lost tons of weight and the last time that Rose had seen her, she had looked almost skeletal.

"Oh, she's gaining a bit of weight now. I think she's getting better."

Rose looked over her shoulder. The white car drove by and disappeared down Long Hill.

"Oh, Greg, could you do me a favour, please?" Rose asked anxiously.

"Sure, what is it, Rose?"

"That white car that just drove by, could you call me if you see it again? I was followed by that car and it worries me to think that it might come back again."

"I'll definitely call you if I see it again. But you really should call the police."

Rose walked up to their front door where she was greeted by two very crazy dogs jumping up and down, tails wagging and very pleased to see their mistress.

Tom got back from golf half an hour later. He had eaten lunch at the club house. Rose hadn't eaten anything, but she wasn't overly hungry. She put the kettle on for a pot of tea and got out some crackers and cheese.

"Tom, it's so lovely outside, do you fancy going for a nice walk, maybe to the Woodland Trail? We can let Puff and Ben off their leashes, and we could check out the Croquet Club. We haven't been there since last October. Oh, and by the way, Jean and Mike have invited us to play a game of croquet with them on Wednesday."

"Yes, well why not. We're so blessed to have such wonderful trails here in Bayfield, everyone should be out walking them. Just give me an hour, love, to rest up before we go walking. I've been on my feet all morning playing golf and I'm not getting any younger."

Rose sat down with a plate of cheese, crackers, and an apple and Tom brought her over a cup of tea. They sat peacefully together in the sunroom along with the two dogs at their feet. Rose had completely forgotten to tell either Tom or Susan about the white car and the Koreans. She would later regret this absent mindedness.

TWENTY-EIGHT

After saying goodbye to Agent Lewis, Susan felt a slight feeling of emptiness. She had enjoyed Andy's company greatly and had even promised to have lunch with him again the next time that he was in Bayfield. It wasn't that she was particularly attracted to him that made Susan feel so strange. Yes, he was handsome and quite disarming in his way, but it was a slight sense of déjà vu. Hadn't she once started up an affair with Jim Reynolds all those years ago and wasn't he too a married man with teenage boys? Susan shook her head and thought, *I am not having an affair, I have just had a perfectly good business lunch with a fellow colleague and nothing more.*

Susan left The Little Inn and drove down Catherine Street onto Bayfield Terrace and down to Rose and Tom's house. There were no cars in the driveway. Had she arrived just a few minutes earlier she would have seen Puff and Ben jump into the old Volvo, followed by Rose and Tom. *Oh well,* thought Susan, *I'll come back later.* She had a lot of tidying up to do back at her condo from the night before. Thinking about her evening with Peter Joyce Susan suddenly felt extremely guilty. Here she was analysing her feelings for Andy Lewis when Peter was most definitely the man in her life. Sometimes Susan, she said to herself, you act like an adolescent teenager. Agent Lewis is a married man and that is the way it was going to stay.

Tom pulled the car up to the Croquet Club car park. There was no one around, nobody playing croquet, in fact it was eerily peaceful. They let the dogs out and didn't even bother to put them on their leashes. They set off down the trail with Puff and Ben running ahead sniffing at everything they passed.

First, they turned left and walked past a farmhouse where horses were grazing lazily on pastures green. Rose called the dogs over; she didn't want them to spook the horses. After leaving the farm, the real trail began, and it was quite strenuous. The trail path had been cut into the sides of natural hills and wooden planks formed rough hewn steps up and down the troughs and hills. A few black flies were out, and Rose flicked them away. They were silent biters but hurt afterwards like sharp stings.

Ben stopped running and stood still, his one paw curled up in question, his whole body alert. He had obviously heard something and was on the defensive. *It was probably a rabbit*, Rose thought, yet she followed his line of sight. One minute Rose was standing up then next second she felt her whole body jolt backwards as she was hurled to the ground with such force that all air was sucked out of her lungs.

"What was that?" was all she could say and then all around her everything blurred, and her last thoughts were, *if I am dead then this isn't too bad...*

Tom, who had walked on ahead with Puff, heard a whooshing sound and Rose say, "What was that?" but when he turned around, at first he could not see Rose. Ben had charged back the way they had come and was barking like a mad dog at something, and Puff turned and followed him. *Where was Rose*, he thought as he retraced his steps back the way he had come.

She was lying face down like a crumpled pile of clothing half hidden beneath a scrubby plant. Tom ran and gently turned her over feeling his own heart lurch and his breath coming out in gulps.

"Rose, darling Rose, no this can't be happening, Rose." Tom cradled Rose in his arms and was rocking her while crying at the same time. Suddenly he heard another whooshing sound followed by a crack as a bullet lodged itself into the trunk of a tree barely six inches away from where Tom sat with Rose in his arms. Ben and Puff were still going crazy snarling and barking. He pulled out his cell phone and with a shaky hand he punched in 911.

"Which service do you require?" The dispatch officer said and then proceeded to ask Tom a string of questions which Tom would never remember what he answered because all the while he was anticipating being shot at again. The dogs suddenly stopped their endless barking, and everything went very quiet. Tom stroked Rose's hair and looked more closely at the wound where she had been shot. Her shoulder was oozing blood although her T-shirt covered the actual wound. Rose fluttered her eye lids and moved her head as she whispered Tom's name.

"Tom, what happened?"

"Shh...my darling, don't try to speak. You're going to be alright. Help is coming." He continued stroking her hair and praying that the paramedics would be able to find them alright in the woods. He had explained that they were about a quarter of the way into the Woodland Trail. Tom wondered where the dogs had gone and had the gunman also left?

As if in answer to his thoughts Ben came charging over followed closely by a limping Puff. Tom was shocked to see blood trickling from the dog's front leg. He called Puff over and examined the wound. Fortunately, it did not look too bad, it was a superficial cut. He made Puff lie down and rest next to Rose who had started to shiver uncontrollably.

"I'm cold, Tom, dreadfully cold."

She's in shock, Tom thought as he called both dogs over to lie next to their mistress. He didn't have a jacket on otherwise he would have covered Rose to keep her warm. Instead, he cradled her closer to his own body. Rose closed her eyes and Tom didn't know whether she had gone to sleep or if she was unconscious.

Finally, twenty minutes later, Tom heard sirens coming down David Street getting louder and louder as they approached the Croquet Club. Puff and Ben barked when three paramedics appeared followed by what looked like a whole arsenal of police wearing helmets and protective vests, their guns out ready.

The paramedics took charge and soon Rose was laid out on a stretcher tucked under a foil blanket, a saline drip attached to her arm.

"Are you alright, sir?" a paramedic asked Tom looking at him closely and taking note of the blood splattered all over his clothing.

"Oh, I'm fine, just a bit shaken. I'll follow you out and then quickly drop our dogs off at our house. Are you taking my wife to Clinton or Goderich?"

"She will be taken straight away to Clinton Emergency. Join us there as soon as you can, sir."

Tom grabbed the dog's leashes and clipped them on. His legs felt decidedly rubbery. The shock of what had just happened had begun to click in.

As soon as Susan heard the news, she dashed over to Clinton hospital. She arrived just after Rose had been wheeled out of surgery and into a ward. Tom was at her side, his hand holding her hand as she slept the deep sleep of someone anaesthetized.

Susan ran up to Tom and gave him a hug. She looked at him and saw shock and exhaustion written all over his face.

"It was horrible, Susan," he said. "A nightmare. I thought that I'd lost her." His eyes welled up and he shook his head trying to get a grip.

'Is she going to be alright?" Susan asked.

Tom ran his hands through his hair and let out a big sigh.

"They removed the bullet from her shoulder. It narrowly missed a main artery. Oh my God, she was so lucky. The surgeon says that she should make a good recovery."

"Thank goodness for that. Look, Rose is going to be out for the count. Let's grab a cup of coffee at Tim Horton's. We can bring it back here and then we can talk. If you don't want to leave her, I'll go and bring back some coffee here, but we have to talk, Tom."

Tom seemed reluctant to leave Rose and so Susan left and was back within ten minutes. Rose was still unconscious.

"Now, Tom," Susan said as she handed him a coffee, "Can you tell me exactly what happened?"

Susan opened her notebook and started to write as Tom related the events leading up to the shooting. He was just concluding his statement when Dr. Jacob's came in to check on Rose. He introduced himself and said, "You might as well go home, Tom, as your wife will be out for at least another eight hours. We've done all that we can for her, she just must let her body heal and sleep is the best medicine. The nurses will dress the wound and, in all likelihood, providing there is no infection, she will be allowed home tomorrow. Go home and get some sleep, you look exhausted."

Tom kissed Rose on her forehead and left the ward with Susan at his side. When they got to his car she said, "Tom, are you sure that you're okay? Look, I'm going to send a police officer around to keep watch over your house. These men are out to get you and

Rose, and they will most certainly return. It could be that you might be better off going to the safe house like Lora."

Tom blanched at the memory of their interrogation at the safe house in London. Absolutely no way did he want to go back there again.

"Look, Susan, I'll be alright. The dogs need to be fed and walked. I do appreciate your offer of police protection though. Now, I must go before I drop."

Susan gave him a hug and watched as he slowly drove away. She then went back inside the hospital to ask the administration if she could send a police officer in to sit outside the ward where Rose was sleeping. There were assassins out there who would stop at nothing.

Tom arrived home twenty minutes later and was greeted by two very hungry and very anxious dogs. He couldn't believe the time. It was already nine o'clock at night. The shooting had taken place around 2:30 p.m.; Tom had been at the hospital for over six hours. After he had fed Puff and Ben, Tom opened the fridge to see what he could find to eat himself.

There was a small bowl of left-over spaghetti pie and some salad. He poured himself out a glass of red wine and sat down to eat. At ten o'clock he rang the hospital and they informed him that Rose was still sleeping. He looked at his watch and decided that it was probably too late to call the kids. He would wait until morning. Wearily, Tom went to bed and the minute his head hit the pillow he was out like a light.

om woke up with a start at six, jumped out of bed and telephoned the hospital. Rose was awake and wanting to see him. He dressed quickly, grabbed a bowl of cereal and a cup of tea, let the dogs out, gave them some kibble and was on the road to Clinton hospital by 6:30 a.m. Had he not been in such a hurry he might have noticed a white car following him, but as it was, he pulled into the hospital car park and ran into the visitors lounge oblivious of his followers.

Rose was sitting up in bed looking very pale, but quite alert. She had a bandage around her shoulder and chest, over which a hospital robe had been loosely draped. There were dark shadows under her eyes which made her look very frail and vulnerable.

"Oh, Tom, I woke up and you weren't here, and I didn't know where you were!"

Tom sat on the chair next to the hospital bed and took Rose's hand.

"They sent me home, love. You were dead to the world. Anyhow, how does your shoulder feel? The doctor said that it was a clean shot, just missed a main artery, but your recovery should be good. You gave me one hell of a fright."

Rose's eyes welled up with tears.

"It all happened so fast, Tom. One minute I was enjoying our walk, the next I felt myself being catapulted backwards to the ground. Did the police catch the gunman?"

"No, even though it looked like an army of police that responded to my 911 call, quite scary, all dressed up in their protective black bullet proof vests and helmets. I suppose they were a SWAT team, but where they came from at such short notice is beyond me. I was asked loads of questions though, but the bottom line is that Puff and Ben chased the assassins off. They are our heroes, love, they saved our lives."

"Oh Tom, did they shoot at you as well?"

"Yes, but the bullet missed, and the dogs went crazy snarling and barking. Anyway, don't dwell on it, love, we're both okay. The doctor says that you can go home today."

Rose smiled and then let out a long yawn. With a very sleepy voice she said, "Darling, I'm going back to sleep now. Will you come back for me later?"

"Yes, love, I'll check with the doctors first but in all likelihood, I'll be back early afternoon. Now sleep tight, my love. I love you."

"Tom, have you told the kids? I don't want to alarm them, I'm really alright."

"Don't worry yourself, love. I'll give them a call when I get back home. Now you really do need to sleep."

Rose closed her eyes and Tom got up to leave when suddenly she opened her eyes again and grabbed Tom's hand urgently,

"Tom, please, oh please, give those coded papers to Susan. I am convinced that the Korean's are after them." Rose then closed her eyes again and within seconds was sound asleep.

Tom got up, found the doctor in charge who was in the middle of his rounds, and asked him about Rose. Fortunately, he had already checked in on her and was more than happy with her progress. He told Tom that she could go back home that afternoon.

Returning to his car, Tom drove off and headed back towards Bayfield. He had just driven past Elliot's Liquidation Warehouse when he noticed a white car behind him driving way too close. Suddenly, without warning, the white car accelerated and over-took Tom only to stop right in front of his vehicle causing Tom to slam his foot down hard on the breaks.

"What the fuck?" Tom yelled.

It all happened so quickly that afterwards Tom could barely put together the order of events. A man got out of the white car holding a rifle which he aimed at Tom. Tom grabbed his steering wheel and pulled it around causing the car to spin until it was actually facing the way that he had just driven. Tom pushed his foot hard down on the accelerator and drove off back into Clinton and onto Highway 8 to Vanastra hoping that a Police car would stop him for speeding. He sped out onto the Varna Road and kept up his speed unimpeded all the way to Mill Street.

He could not see any white car in his rear mirror at all. Tom slowed down when he reached Bayfield. He drove up to Bayfield Terrace only to find cars and vans parked all along the roadside leading to their home. There was a CBC van parked in his driveway and radio station vans all parked in front of the house. A camera man filming the entranceway turned his camera on Tom as he pulled up his car into the driveway. A CBC news anchorman ran up to him with his microphone thrust out at Tom.

"Mr. Blair, Tom, isn't it? Can you tell us how your wife is doing? We understand that she was involved in a shootout on the Woodland Trail..." And so it went on. Tom pushed past all the press and opened the front door. He was greeted by Puff and Ben. He went straight into the living room and got out his cell phone, punching in Susan Parker's number. He looked at the time. It was only 9:00 a.m. and Susan would be in the middle of her team meeting. He decided to leave her a text message.

Susan arrived at The Lions Hall bang on 8:00 a.m. Her team were waiting and eager to hear all about the shooting.

"Good morning everyone. Well, much has happened since we last met yesterday. As you have all heard, Rose Blair was shot and wounded while walking the Woodland Trail with Tom and their two dogs. The bullet is with Forensics right now, but I have no doubt about who the assassins are - the Koreans. I have here the Emergency Response team's report and the SWAT team's report. What does intrigue me, however, is how the SWAT team got to the crime scene so fast. According to the report prior to Tom Blair phoning in for help at 2:45 p.m. the SWAT team received a call at 2:35 pm saying that some snipers were in the Woodland Trail following the Blairs. Now, how would anyone know that unless they had been trailing Rose and Tom themselves and had seen the gunmen?"

As Susan said these words it suddenly occurred to her that maybe CSIS had been following Rose and Tom. She would have to make sure by phoning Agent Lewis and asking him point blank what was going on.

She focused back on her team.

"If it was the Koreans, and I repeat that I am pretty certain that it was, they are obviously out to kill the Blairs. These are mercenaries who will stop at nothing to fulfil their contract. We are still unsure of the motive, but it appears that the Du Preez's were tied up with some heavy espionage work and it could be that whatever they stumbled upon, some project, the Koreans needed to silence them before they told the whole world."

Susan was aware that she had almost given away the fact that the Du Preez's were actually Mossad agents. Agent Lewis had made her promise not to reveal this, but it was very difficult not to give too much away. She returned to her narrative.

"This is only speculation at best. We don't really have too much to go on, but it does add up to one reason why the Du Preez's might have been murdered."

Sergeant Flowers interrupted.

'But, Ma'am, why are the Blairs their target now?"

Susan answered the Sergeant quickly.

"Because of the multiple burglaries not only at the Du Preez home in Windhoek, but their daughter's apartment in New York and now Rose and Tom also had their house broken into, it all indicates that someone, somewhere is looking for something and it must be pretty darn important to kill for. We think that the Du Preez's have hidden vital information somewhere and it could be the Blair's are unwittingly holding this information. It could be of national or even international importance.

"Now, I want around the clock surveillance on the Blair's, not only their home, but they must be watched wherever they go. Their lives are truly at risk."

Sergeant Mathieson stood up to speak. "Shouldn't they go to a safe house like the daughter? That would be the safest place for them."

"Yes, Sergeant, but Tom Blair says that he wants to stay put in Bayfield. We cannot force them to go."

"Well, CSIS managed to force Lora Du Preez against her will, why can't we do the same?"

Susan felt her voice and blood pressure rise.

"Sergeant , we are not a Police State and we do not go around coercing people against their will. Rose and Tom are not criminals, they are decent, hardworking, and caring people who deserve to be treated with the utmost respect and dignity. Now, team, you must all be on extreme alert and be totally vigilante. We are looking for a white car, we think a Ford Focus, driven by two Koreans. Go out and talk to people and keep your eyes and ears open. I want you all carrying your pistols. These men are armed and dangerous. Now go to it and bring me some results. Same time tomorrow."

The men were dismissed and wandered out of the Lions building while Susan typed up her report. She glanced at her cell phone and realized that Tom had left three text messages. She would get back to him after she had spoken to Agent Lewis. She tapped in Andrew's number from the business card he had given to her, and he answered right away with a crisp, business-like tone.

"Agent Lewis speaking."

"Oh, hi, Andy, it's Susan Parker here, I mean Detective Susan Parker. I do hope you can clear up some issue for me. Did you have Rose and Tom Blair followed yesterday and did one of your people make a call to the SWAT team?"

There was a silence at the other end of the line and then Andy answered.

"Yes to both of your questions."

"I thought so," Susan said. "But why did you have them followed in the first place? I thought that we had established that Rose and Tom were harmless."

"Susan, in our business we don't trust anyone. It's the first rule of the Agency, don't trust anything or take anything at face value. Yes, I know that Rose and Tom are probably just innocent pawns in a complicated game, but they could still lead us to the end result."

Susan was shocked, "So you mean to say you are prepared to risk their lives in order to solve the case?"

"Well... put it that way it doesn't sound too good, but you know I have their backs covered. After all, I did call the SWAT team over to them pretty fast and that probably saved their lives."

"No, it did not. Their dogs saved their lives. Now, Agent Lewis, back off can you, back off or keep me totally in the loop."

"Oh, Detective, I love it when you get angry. No, seriously, I promise to communicate directly with you. I still want to have the Blair's kept on surveillance but believe me we will intervene again should we see anything untoward. Look upon us as an extra pair of hands. Are we friends again?"

Susan couldn't help herself smiling. The man was annoyingly disarming.

"Yes, and I suppose I do owe you an apology for being so rude. This case is really trying my nerves."

"Actually, I'm going to be down in Bayfield on Thursday. Do you fancy meeting for lunch, strictly business? We could exchange notes."

Susan grinned at the thought of having lunch again with Andrew.

"Yes, why not. The Little Inn, say at 12:30 p.m.?"

They said their goodbyes and then Susan's phone rang almost immediately after she had put it away. It was Tom Blair sounding extremely agitated.

"I've been trying to reach you all morning. Can you come over, there are press people everywhere, it's dreadful, but apart from that, I've got something to show you."

Susan said that she would be over after she had grabbed something to eat.

THIRTY

Tom had come back from the hospital and stormed into the house furious with the bombardment of press outside. He had let the dogs outside and finally calmed himself down enough to make a pot of coffee. He really felt like something much stronger, but at 10:30 a.m. he couldn't quite go that far.

Tom had just sat down in the sunroom with a steaming mug of coffee, Ben and Puff at his feet, when the phone rang. He looked to see who was calling. It was Jessica.

"Dad, Dad, is Mom alright? I've just been watching the CBC news and they said that a woman had been shot in Bayfield and then there was a picture of you walking into the house. Why didn't you tell me?"

Tom did feel guilty that their daughter should hear about the shooting on the news. He just hadn't had the time to phone the kids, so much had happened in such a short time.

"I'm really sorry, love, but your mother is doing alright. In fact, she's coming home today. Don't worry, she was really lucky. It was a clean shot."

"Dad, what on earth is going on in Bayfield? First mom and you are plastered all over Facebook and now you're on the National news with Mom being shot. I don't understand any of it."

Tom could hear the worry in his daughter's voice, but there was little he could do other than to placate her with soothing platitudes.

"Look, Jess, bad things happen, but the good news is that your mother is going to be okay. I will get her to phone you when she gets back home from the hospital, hopefully this afternoon. Now I must go, love."

No sooner had Tom put the phone down when it rang again. This time it was Anne from Halifax.

"Dad, Dad, I just heard on the news about the shooting in Bayfield. Dad, Mom is alright, isn't she?"

Tom went through the whole spiel again. In future, he thought, he would make sure that his children knew everything before the media vultures descended.

As he said his goodbyes to Anne, he almost expected the phone to ring again with Paul on the line. But it didn't and he was spared having to go over the details for a third time. Tom did, however, send Paul a text message saying that his mother was fine and not to worry.

His coffee was cold by the time he got back to the sunroom. Tom picked up his mug and took it to the microwave where he gave it a quick zap. He looked at the kitchen clock and realized that Susan would be over shortly. First, he wanted to look at the decoded paper and see if he could make head or tails out of it. Rose had thought that some of the deciphering referred to map coordinates, so Tom grabbed an atlas from the study.

He opened the atlas to the map of the world. Glancing at the decoded numbers and letters he immediately saw what Rose had spotted. 24.5700S 17.0836E, the lines of longitude and latitude.

He could see on the map that the same coordinates took him to the Namib Desert in Namibia just 100 km from Windhoek and 20 km outside the town of Okahandja close to the Van Bach Dam. Reading the jumble of letters Tom read, RTZ and then the letters and numbers U238, 90% U235. The first of the numbers looked like calculations.

Tom wrote out all the words that he could decipher and the map coordinates. He would hand this and the original coded papers over to Susan.

The barrage of press had thinned out considerably by the time Susan arrived. There were just the CBC crew and a couple of the local radio stations. Tom looked out the window and saw Susan put her hand up in a gesture saying, "No." He opened the front door slightly letting her squeeze in. No way did he want to be recorded on television again.

"Thank you for coming, Susan. I have to tell you how exasperating this all is having the media camped on our doorstep."

"By the end of the day, Tom, they'll have gone onto another story. What time are you leaving to bring Rose home?"

"Well, that's what I wanted to talk to you about," Tom said, his voice taking on a serious note.

"You see, I was followed today, and another attempt was made on my life. I was driving back from the hospital when a white car pulled out in front of me, and a man pulled out a gun. I managed to do a wheelie and drove like a maniac back to Bayfield via Varna and Mill Road."

Susan interrupted him. "You did say a white car? Was it driven by two Asians?"

"Yes, I think that it was a Ford Focus, new looking, but my main concern is that they might try to shoot again when I go to collect Rose. I cannot have that happen to her. I have two favours to ask of you."

Tom looked at Susan with desperate eyes. This man, Susan thought, had been to hell and back and was still in the middle of his nightmare. She answered him, "Go on, Tom, what do you want me to do? You know that I'm here to help you both as a friend and a professional."

Tom sighed and continued. "Do you think that you could pick Rose up discreetly, maybe park your car at the rear of the hospital and get her in the car from the rear exit? I will still drive over to so called *visit* Rose and I'll ask the nursing staff to let it be known that Rose will be staying in hospital for a few more days. If you could keep your Police Officer on watch in front of her room, then the assassins will be under the impression that she is still in hospital. My second favour is, could Rose move in with you for a few days? I feel that even with police protection we are still most vulnerable in our own house. I will stay on by myself and maybe we can force their hands by provoking them somehow. I don't know how, but I just don't want Rose to be party to any more violence."

Susan nodded in agreement.

"Yes, of course she can move in with me for a few days. I'll make up the guest room, but Tom, are you sure that both of you wouldn't be better off in the safe house in London?"

Tom shook his head, "No, I'm not going to be driven out of my own home by those thugs. I do have to admit to being somewhat frightened, but I have Puff and Ben here and they already saved our lives once."

"Well, Tom, we will have around the clock surveillance for you, but don't try anything without discussing it with me first. I'd rather that you stayed close to home, don't go out to play golf or croquet, it's too risky being out in the open in plain view of any sniper. Right, so what time should I pick up Rose?"

They agreed a time and then, almost like an afterthought, Tom said, "Now Susan, I've got something important to show you." He went over to the kitchen table and handed her the two sheets of paper with the four columns of numbers.

"These were found in Rose's carry-on suitcase tucked into the lining. Well, one sheet was in the lining, the other sheet was in an envelope addressed to us which Lora Du Preez brought with her from New York. You see, it looks as if Andre and Jan were fearful that these papers might get into the wrong hands. It also looks at if this was all premeditated."

Susan looked at the row of numbers and whistled.

"Wow! Do you know what this means, Tom?"

"No, well, yes and no. Lora grew up in a house where her parents were forever leaving her cryptic messages. She looked at these numbers and helped us decipher the code."

Tom pulled out the third sheet of paper with Rose's hand-written words and the co-ordinates listed. He handed it over to Susan.

"Look, Susan, this is what we've learned." He pointed to the coordinates and then pulled up a map of the world on his iPhone. He showed her the co-ordinates and pointed to the map which showed the GPS reading close to Windhoek, Namibia.

"I still don't know what it all means, but I'm sure your friends in CSIS will be able to analyse this. It's my belief that this is what those Koreans have been prepared to kill for so please take them off my hands."

Susan smiled, "You know, Tom, I think that Rose and you have finally found the motive for all these burglaries and murders. I'll pass this on to Agent Lewis at CSIS."

"Agent Lewis, do you know him personally, Susan?"

"Well, we've discussed this case and I challenged him over the drone. You will be pleased to know that you're no longer prime suspects."

"That's a relief," Tom said. "Does that mean that the drone will go?"

"No, I'm afraid they're keeping up the surveillance but that's for your own good, Tom."

Tom thought for a minute. "Susan, we need to draw the Korean's out once and for all. This cat and mouse game must stop. Now that you in effect have joined forces with CSIS surely it will be much easier to apprehend these men."

"Yes and no Tom. The Koreans will have switched cars by now so it will be useless looking for a white Ford Focus. Also, even though we have reached an impasse with the CSIS team we both have set protocols to follow. Don't you worry, we will find these men. There is a full-scale red alert out for them. They will not be able to go far. Now, I need to get these very important papers off to CSIS and copied to my Chief. I am sure that this will prove to be something huge on an international scale so, be prepared for the paparazzi descending upon you again."

"Okay, Susan, so I'll come around to your condo this afternoon after I've made sure that I haven't been followed. I will call Rose at the hospital and explain our plan to her.

Susan left holding the papers in her hand. She would have to deal with it straight away as it was like holding an explosive bomb, one which could go off at any time soon.

THIRTY-ONE

Rose listened to Tom carefully. She understood the need for secrecy but, all the same, she felt uncomfortable with all the cloak and dagger charades. She hoped that the Koreans would soon be caught.

Having had time on her side by being confined to her hospital bed, Rose had spent some time Googling the country of Namibia. She learned quite a lot.

Windhoek was the capital city, and the country was bound by the Atlantic on the West side, Angola and Zambia to the North, Botswana to the East and South Africa to the South.

Thirty percent of Namibia to the northeast was the Kalahari Desert, another twenty percent was the Namib Desert, the Okavango swamps in the North and most of the South West was buried under huge sand dunes.

The country sounded terribly inhospitable and why anyone would choose to live there was beyond Rose's imagination.

Namibia was, however, very rich in natural resources with gold, diamonds, uranium, and many other base metals. There was a huge uranium mining corporation owned by the British just outside the town of Okahandja.

At the mention of uranium, Rose Googled to find out more on the subject. The letters and numbers U235 and U238 jumped out at her. Had she not seen those same numbers on the decoded print out? It soon became very clear as Rose read on that enrichment plants for Uranium could possibly be found at the co-ordinates written on the decoded sheets.

It was an enlightened moment for Rose when she slotted the pieces of information together like a jigsaw puzzle. The North Korean's were making or planning to make weapons of mass destruction in the deserts of Namibia.

This must have been what the Du Preez's had discovered and were killed for. If the Koreans thought that Tom and Rose knew this information, it now made sense why they wanted to have them eliminated.

It all became crystal clear to Rose, the burglaries, the shootings, and the stalking. She was relatively safe in the hospital, but now, Rose wasn't so sure about leaving. Maybe Tom and she should join Lora at the safe house in London, Rose thought as she picked up her cell phone to call Tom.

Susan tapped in Agent Lewis's cell number. She waited impatiently for him to pick it up.

"Andrew, thank goodness you answered, I have something really important to show you. I know that CSIS and Interpol will be very interested. Is there any chance that you could come to Bayfield soon as I'm loathed to fax this to you? It's just far too important."

"Susan, I'm actually in London at the safe house visiting Lora Du Preez right now. I can be with you in just over an hour."

Susan looked at her watch. She had promised to pick Rose up from the hospital in an hour. She thought quickly.

"Andrew, have you had any lunch yet? I could meet you at The Black Dog and if I'm a bit late you can just go ahead and order something to eat. I may be about 20 minutes late."

With that sorted out Susan looked around her living room and decided to quickly run the vacuum over the carpet. She had made up the guest room and cleaned the bathroom. It had been a long time since she had had any guests to stay.

Arriving at the hospital half an hour later Susan drove to the back of the building and entered through the rear doors normally used for deliveries. Susan was horrified at the lack of security. Anyone could have entered the hospital as there was no screening.

Tom would probably either be on his way over or he might even be already upstairs with Rose right now, Susan thought as she took the elevator to the second floor. Tom had agreed to meet up at Susan's condo later that afternoon.

Rose was sitting up in bed looking much better than the last time Susan had seen her. She smiled as her friend entered the room. The police officer who had been posted outside Rose's room also smiled and nodded his head as a greeting to Susan as she closed the door behind her.

"Hi Rose, Tom spoke to you about our plans, didn't he?" Susan asked anxiously.

"Oh, yes, thank you for offering to have me stay with you for a few days. To be honest Tom and I should be going to the safe house in London, you know it would be much easier for everyone if we did."

"Yes, well I did suggest that to him, Rose, but he is rather stubborn. He refuses to be intimidated."

Rose laughed. "Tell me about it, Tom Blair is one of the most stubborn people that I know. Now, he should be here quite soon although he did say not to wait for him. He's pretending to visit me, so I expect he'll be back in Bayfield quite shortly after we get to your place."

"Yes, he's probably on his way here right now. I'll give you a few minutes to get dressed and ready to go. Do you need any help with dressing with your shoulder?"

"No, I think that I can manage okay, but thanks for asking. Just give me five minutes."

Ten minutes later Susan was on the road again with Rose sitting in the passenger seat. Hopefully they would be back home in fifteen minutes, Rose thought suddenly feeling very fatigued.

THIRTY-TWO

Tom set off to Clinton in a cheery mood. It was another beautiful day with a clear, cloudless blue sky. At first his was the only vehicle on the road and it remained the case until he reached Porters Hill Line. A black Lexus pulled out behind him. The windows were tinted so Tom was unable to clearly see the driver and passenger.

He smiled to himself thinking that he could easily guess that it was the CSIS agents following him. Susan had told him that they would continue their surveillance on them for their own protection. He was a bit concerned, though, when the Black Lexus almost rammed into the back of him. He put his foot down on the accelerator and raced forward. The Lexus suddenly overtook him and then, just like the time before, it stopped right in front of him, and Tom was forced to slam on his brakes.

Barely had he stopped when two Koreans jumped out of the Lexus, pulled open Tom's driver side door, and dragged him out. They put duct tape over his mouth and then wound duct tape around his wrists. Tom tried to kick but his legs were soon grabbed and then between the two of them they dragged him over to their car and threw him into the trunk.

They drove off at top speed leaving Tom's Volvo in the middle of the road with the driver's door wide open. The abduction had taken barely one minute to conduct.

Tom lay in the darkness of the trunk. He wriggled his wrists and soon had one hand loosened from the tape. Finally, both hands were free. Tom pulled the tape off his mouth wincing as it yanked at his skin. He pulled out his cell phone and punched in Susan's number. She picked up a few moments later.

"Detective Parker speaking?"

"I'm in the trunk of a black Lexus driven by the Koreans! They pulled out in front of me again just past Porter's Line. I'm not sure where we are right now."

"Tom, use the cell's GPS. I can't be that far away from you. I'll call for back up."

The Lexus suddenly turned right onto Airport Road. Tom was thrown around in the trunk of the car. He managed to use his cell phone to call again. Susan picked up straight away.

"Tom, stay on the phone as we are tracking you through your phone. I have a whole team following the car you're in. It looks as if you might be headed for London, no, wait..." Susan saw the Lexus take a right turn onto Mill Road, "it looks like they're heading back into Bayfield. Now, Tom, just remember the car is surrounded. When they stop, I don't want any heroics. You must stay in the trunk, do you understand?"

Tom, who had always slightly suffered from claustrophobia, wiped the sweat off his brow and tried to stop hyperventilating. He quietly asked Susan if he could speak to Rose.

Rose, who was sitting next to Susan, had overheard everything. Susan, who had been talking through her hands-free device nodded to Rose to speak.

"Tom, Tom, my love, you must do what Susan says and don't try anything. These men are dangerous. Oh, love, please be careful. I love you."

Tom, lying curled up in the trunk of the Lexus, suddenly felt very alone and emotional. It was hearing Rose's voice that did it. He gulped back his emotions and whispered into the phone.

"Rose, my love, I just want you to know how much I love you. You are my everything."

"Oh, Tom, love, don't worry, we'll get you home alright, just stay calm."

Rose could hear the level of panic rising in Tom's voice. She also knew how he hated confined spaces, even just going up into the attic of their house made him feel uncomfortable, so what he must be feeling being trapped in the trunk of the car was unimaginable. *My poor, poor, darling Tom,* Rose thought as she tried to reassure the man she loved that everything would be okay.

Susan took over the conversation.

"Tom, you've reached Bayfield and I'm just one car behind you. The Lexus is turning right onto Main Street, keep this line open. I'm just putting in a call through to Agent Lewis."

Susan punched in Andrew's cell number. He would be on his way to Bayfield by now.

He answered curtly, "Agent Lewis speaking."

"Andrew, we've got a red alert here. Tom Blair has been abducted by the Koreans. He is in the trunk of a black Lexus license plate Bravo Delta Whiskey Romeo six two four. I'm following them and we have the whole team out. Could you send some back up people too?"

There was a silence while Andrew thought and then he answered. "I can send the Agents manning the surveillance drone on Colina Street and I am in Varna, so will be able to join you soon. Keep me posted."

The Lexus drove over the bridge, past the Docks and then turned left towards the Marina. Susan followed a small distance behind. She called the team on the radio and gave them the location and then she contacted the CSIS agents to let them also know where the Lexus was headed.

It pulled in at the end of the Marina access where normally boats were loaded or lifted into the water. There was a sleek, black power boat tied up to the docks.

When Rose saw the boat, she immediately explained to Susan that she had noticed it moored there for the past week.

Suddenly the two Koreans jumped out of the car and, with one quick movement, had opened the trunk and dragged Tom out before Susan and her team had any time to gear into action. They then jumped onto the speed boat with Tom kicking and trying to get away. They started up the engine and prepared to leave the docks.

"Oh, no," Susan cried. "They're getting away. Coast guard, call the Coast Guard!" she shouted into her phone to the dispatch operator.

Andrew Lewis pulled his car in behind Susan's and jumped out, running to her and shouting to her as he ran.

"Quick, this way, Susan, CSIS has a boat moored over by Cottage Colony. Follow me."

Rose, who had watched with horror as Tom was dragged and thrown onto the black speed boat, geared into action. She ran after Susan and Andrew whom she had never met before but appeared to be obviously in command of the situation. Not to mention, tall and handsome.

They arrived at the Cottage Colony with Rose lagging behind completely out of breath. She really should go back to her fitness classes, Rose thought as she stood for a minute trying to catch her breath. Susan and Andrew had already jumped onto a white speed boat.

"Wait for me," Rose yelled and leapt onto the boat just as Andrew was casting off. Susan gunned the throttle and Rose was thrown backwards as the small boat sped forward.

They could see the black boat opening throttle as it reached the lake.

"Quick, oh quick, we have to catch up to them!" Rose shouted while she watched with a sinking heart as the sleek black boat gained speed and disappeared off into the horizon.

THIRTY-THREE

Tom looked around. He was aboard a very powerful boat, of that he was sure. The two Koreans were focused on piloting and steering the boat out of the harbour and were not actually watching Tom. He knew that generally flare guns and other safety items were kept under the passenger seats. How could he open one of the seats without drawing attention to himself?

He would have to distract them for a minute to give himself enough time to grab something that he could use. Tom bent down and slid off one of his shoes. Would they even hear it plop into the water if he threw it? Probably not, as the sound of the engines combined with the water being sprayed up would most certainly drown out any noise completely. What else could he do?

Tom thought. If he could cause the engine to stall that might keep them both occupied enough to buy him some time. He looked back at the two massive outboard motors churning up a huge wake as it sped along the lake. If he threw his shoe at the engine would that do the trick? *It was worth the try,* Tom thought to himself, *nothing ventured, nothing gained.*

When the Koreans were looking the other way, Tom aimed his shoe directly at one of the propellers. He heard a sick thud and then the engine spluttered and the boat stopped. The two Korean's ran over and looked at the engines. One of them pulled the propeller up out of the water and frowned. The other man jabbered away at him in Korean while Tom inched his fingers under the seat and gently started to lift it up.

There was no easy way to do it. He would just have to raise the seat and hopefully grab whatever his hands could find. He did exactly that and was fortunate enough to find his hand around a flare gun. Just as he raised it up one of the Koreans yelled out a warning. Tom fired as the Korean charged forward. The flare gun went off at point blank range and blew a hole in the Korean's chest. The other Korean, seeing this grabbed his pistol aiming it at Tom. Tom, using the empty flare gun, tried unsuccessfully to knock the pistol away. Tom dove overboard just as the Korean fired, missing him by mere inches.

It all happened so fast. Tom didn't have time to think. He dove under the icy water, ignoring the frigid temperature and swam as far away as his lungs would allow before he cautiously came up for air. As he surfaced, his heart beat like a drum, but the sight of a small white boat speeding in his direction gave him hope. The black boat was still close enough to be fired at so Tom gulped some more air and once again dove under water just as another shot was fired at him. He prayed that he could put in enough distance away from the boat so that he would be out of the line of fire.

Rose, meanwhile, urged Andrew to make the boat go faster. She had witnessed Tom diving overboard and then, to her horror, had seen him being shot at.

Suddenly they heard the sound of a helicopter getting closer and closer. It was the Canadian Coast Guard.

Tom swam as fast as he could towards the speeding white boat.

He heard the gun man shooting but this time it was not aimed at him. He looked up to the sky and could see a helicopter closing in on the black boat. For himself he was too exhausted and wasn't quite sure how much further he could go.

Just as Tom was flagging, there was an almighty explosion. He dared to look backwards to where the black speed boat had been. To his horror there was an inferno of fire. The helicopter was still hovering overhead, and he could see the pilot and his passenger scanning the lake for survivors.

Suddenly, the white speed boat pulled in alongside Tom with Rose crying out to him to grab the side. He was pulled into the boat by a tall man the likes of which he had never seen before who introduced himself to Tom as Agent Lewis. Rose and Susan hugged him, and they returned to the Marina.

On the docks, Tom could see an ambulance and three police cars with their lights flashing. The SWAT team had been called out and the whole Marina had been taped off to the public.

The press had just arrived as Tom, Rose, Susan, and Andrew pulled in and moored the boat. In the crowds of policemen an older man wearing a suit stepped forward.

Susan whispered to Rose, "That's the Chief, my boss." He stepped over to where Rose and Tom were huddled.

"We need to talk immediately. What you gave to Detective Parker is dynamite, but it needs to be verified. I know that this is the last thing that you will want to do right now, but we do need to have this interview before we can proceed."

He looked at Rose with her shoulder and arm bandaged up. Her face looked chalk white and great dark shadows were drawn like half moons beneath her eyes.

"Oh, I'm sorry, ma'am. I totally forgot about your injury. Look, I can interview Tom alone if you like. I promise not to keep him too long. I'll get Detective Parker to take you home."

Rose, who was clinging to Tom said, "No, I want to go with Tom. Let's just get this over with and then we can both go home together."

Susan, who had been deep in conversation with Agent Lewis introduced Tom to him.

"Tom, this is Agent Lewis from CSIS."

Looking at the handsome man before him Tom realized that he himself was getting old. There was a time, he thought, when I might have been considered handsome, but those days were definitely gone. He was just grateful that he and Rose had survived the course and still loved each other very much.

He wasn't sure about Agent Lewis. He seemed a smarmy type, a bit too full of himself. He found himself replying quite curtly.

"Oh, yes, you and your surveillance team. I don't know whether to thank you or to curse you. Rose and I did not appreciate being spied upon. However, I suppose that you've just saved my life so that somewhat evens the score, doesn't it?" Tom said as he shook hands with the Agent.

"Call me Andrew and yes, I do need to apologise for the drone. You were our prime suspects for quite a while you know." Andrew slapped Tom on his back and smiled.

Rose looked at Andrew and then at her friend Susan and absentmindedly thought what a great couple they would make.

Susan, who had been listening to the conversation between the Chief and Tom turned to Rose and said, "Rose, dear Rose, are you quite sure that you don't want me to take you home to rest. You do look exhausted and very pale."

"No, Susan, let's just wrap this all up and then I can rest. Let's just do it, can we?"

Susan smiled. Rose was a just do it kind of gal.

They all drove over to the Lions Hall managing to avoid the

press which they left for Andrew and the rest of the SWAT team to handle.

Driving up to the village everything seemed so normal. Absolutely no one would have known the drama that had just been enacted down at the harbour. Susan unlocked the Lions Hall and the Chief walked in followed by Rose and Tom.

"You know, Susan, this is the first time that I've actually visited your incident room here in Bayfield. Was this originally a classroom?" He said while looking at the chalkboard that spanned the end of the room.

"Why yes, sir, this was the Bayfield Village School. It was built in the 50s and closed in the 70s. It was then used as a Town Hall, then the Lions have used it as their meeting place since the early 90s."

Rose and Tom walked in and immediately their eyes were drawn to the large white board where photographs of Andre and Jan Du Preez and the two Korcan's were posted along with, to their shock, pictures of Lora Du Preez and themselves. Three photographs of different cars were also on the board and then some rather gruesome and very graphic pictures of both Jan and Andre taken at the crime scenes. Rose averted her eyes and Tom gently lead her over to the conference table where they both sat down. The Chief and Susan sat at the head of the table.

"Well, firstly, I have to congratulate you both for finding and deciphering these pieces of paper with all those numbers. Do you know what it all means?"

Rose and Tom both nodded. They felt like students in a classroom. Tom decided to take the lead. "Yes, Rose and I have put the pieces together and what we think is that the Du Preez's found out the location of a Uranium Enrichment plant just outside of a town called Okavango in Namibia. We assume that our Korean friends have something to do with this?"

The Chief looked grim as he said, "Yes, you're right on both counts, but you probably wouldn't have guessed that the Du Preez's were Mossad agents working for the Israelis. They had been watching the British owned uranium mine for a number of years. The frequency of missing shipments of Uranium started escalating, indeed, the British MI6 had also reported the same thing and were investigating on the same level. It appears that the Du Preez's discovered the whereabouts of the uranium enrichment plant, a subterranean operation 20 kilometres outside of Okavango." The Chief paused before continuing.

"Because it was underground it missed the aerial searches that both our agents from CSIS and MI6 agents conducted after being alerted over the missing uranium shipments. Our guess is that the Korean's were on to them. They had to get this vital information out of the country and fast. One of the first rules of espionage is never put all your eggs in one basket. Andre and Jan must have known that their computers were compromised as were their phones."

He coughed and then blew his nose loudly before continuing.

"The only way to get the information out was in stages and in code, hence slipping one sheet of coded numbers in your suitcase lining and then the visit to their daughter. When they planned their visit to you in Bayfield it was to retrieve the piece of paper from your suitcase. Of course, what they did not know was that the Korean's were actually following them and their every move."

Tom interrupted the Chief, "But why did they not just kill them in Windhoek, it seems rather unnecessary following them all the way across the world to end up murdering them here in Bayfield."

The Chief looked at Tom incredulously and then continued, "Tom, they had to know who might have the information hence the burglaries at both their daughter's place and your house. They were looking for the coded pieces of paper."

Rose looked perplexed. "But how did they even know that the Du Preez's had encrypted this information?'

The Chief continued as if he hadn't heard Rose, "There are some things we do not have the answers for yet, but we do know that the Koreans had been watching the Du Preez's for several years now.

We will find out more, I am sure, when the facility in Namibia is raided. The Namibian authorities have been informed and MI6 and CSIS agents have the enrichment plant surrounded. Probably as I speak, the teams will have cordoned off the area.

I hope that you realize that the two of you have potentially stopped some ghastly global terrorism which, had the Korean's succeeded in making nuclear weapons of mass destruction, could have seriously altered the power play of the world as we know it today."

"Wow," Rose said, "Just who would have thought that going on a safari in Kenya would have led to all of this. So, what happens now?"

"Right now, Rose Blair, you need to go home to rest. If you could sign these typed up statements, you will be free to go."

The Chief smiled as he said, "Detective Parker had already sent all the information to me and I got one of the secretaries to type this up. Basically, it is a disclaimer to the effect that you had no prior knowledge of the Du Preez's before meeting them last March on the safari. There is also the matter of the Official Secrets Act which you will need to sign"

Rose looked skeptical, "But of course we didn't know them before, how could we?"

The chief frowned but continued, "For all we know, you could have been in on all of the espionage right from the beginning. No,

I know that you are totally innocent, but for the records we need to have your statements verified and you need to sign the Official Secrets Act."

"Oh, well, I'm sure that you know what you're doing just as long as you do know that Tom and I are innocent. I still feel like a criminal though."

Susan looked at the chief and smiled before saying, "We do know that you and Tom were just being used as pawns and yes, CSIS did totally check you both out and you both came up squeaky clean. Their report on you, however, highlights the fact that you both seemed to be caught up in a number of unfortunate murders taken place here in Bayfield. They do wonder why you should always be in the thick of it."

"And what did you tell them, Susan?" Rose asked feeling a bit shaken by the fact that they had been investigated once again like common criminals.

Susan laughed, "I just told them that you were both the salt of the earth and you never looked for anything but a peaceful life living here in this sleepy, idyllic village of Bayfield."

Tom smiled and put his arms around Rose before he realized with a jolt that her shoulder was still healing and would be incredibly tender.

"Sorry, love, now darling girl..."

Rose interrupted, "Hey Tom, I'm not an invalid, I'll be okay."

Tom continued, "It's time to get you home to bed. You're beginning to look like a panda bear with those large dark circles beneath your eyes."

They shook hands with the Chief and Susan hugged Rose and Tom, "Thank you, dear friends. See you soon."

Tom returned a few minutes later, "Oh, excuse me, Susan, normally we would be happy to walk home, but Rose is about to drop. Could you run us back, please?"

"Oh, I completely forgot you didn't have your car. Of course, I'll run you home. Rose is in no fit state to walk anywhere."

They drove back to Bayfield Terrace in silence. The shock of the afternoon's boat chase and shootings was beginning to hit all three of them, Rose particularly. As she walked into their house being greeted ecstatically by the dogs, she felt her legs buckle beneath her and Tom just caught her before she fainted. He led her gently over to the sofa where Puff and Ben joined her. Tom went to put the kettle on.

"What you need is a strong cup of tea, love, and then it's bed for you."

"Thank you, Tom. Have I told you lately that I love you?"

Much later, after the Chief had departed and Susan had written up her final report, she took down the incident board, wiped the board clean and packed away everything into a box. She had not said her goodbyes to the team, but experience had taught her that by the end of any enquiry everyone was thoroughly burnt out and the time to meet to debrief was normally about one week later. She would call the team together then.

Susan looked at her watch and was shocked to see how late it was. She was supposed to be in London having dinner with Peter Joyce, but it was too late now plus the fact that she was absolutely exhausted.

She drove back to her condo, and as she passed The Docks Susan noticed Agent Andrew Lewis's car parked in the car park.

On the spur of the moment, she pulled over, parked, and went into the bar. It was not busy, and she saw Andrew sitting by himself at the back of the restaurant. She walked over to him and smiled, saying, "I'm paying for the next round..."

A SNEAK PEEK AT MURDER AT THE LITTLE INN!

Rose opened one sleepy eye and looked at the bedside clock. It was eight o'clock and Tom was still sound asleep and gently snoring beside her. Puff and Ben, their beloved dogs, were also asleep, and Rose was sorely tempted to close her eyes and join them in their slumbers. It was, after all, very warm and snug under their feather duvet and why shouldn't she sleep in, except that Rose always felt guilty.

Why she felt this way was beyond her as they were both retired and had earned the right to be lazy. It was probably just conditioning like Pavlov's dogs or something like that, but anyway, today Rose had promised her friend Julie that she would go to the fitness class with her. Julie had been trying to get Rose out to the classes for years and finally, after resisting so long, she had succumbed and had now been going out every Monday, Wednesday, and Friday and had actually loved every bit of it.

Tom also had started pole walking, and he too had attended a few of the early risers' fitness classes aimed at getting men out, about, and fit. Bayfield was, in fact, absolutely brilliant for offering every type of fitness programme available.

There were Tai Chi, yoga, aerobics, pole walking, and occasionally Zumba classes all year round and the instructors were all fantastic.

Once again, Rose felt privileged to be living in the wonderful village of Bayfield.

Lying snug for a few more minutes, still reluctant to get up. Rose made a mental list of what her itinerary was for the day. The most exciting part of the day was going to be the Literary Festival, but that wasn't until the evening.

After the fitness class, Rose had arranged to meet up with Carrie and Jen to have coffee at the Charles Street Market and then home for lunch with Tom. Thinking of food made Rose go through a visual exercise in what they had in the fridge to eat. Not an awful lot, she thought, and so a grocery shop would probably have to feature somewhere in her day's agenda.

Rose finally got up and padded into the kitchen to put the kettle on for a cup of tea. They always started the day with a lovely cuppa. Puff and Ben stretched and followed her into the kitchen, where she let them out into the garden. It felt positively balmy outside; maybe Spring was in the air, although Tom always warned her not to be so optimistic. It was not uncommon to have a dump of snow in April, but at least it rarely settled at that time of the year.

She brought the tea into the bedroom, setting it down on Tom's bedside table. He opened his eyes and looked up at Rose and smiled. "Are you going somewhere, love?"

"I'm off to my fitness class and then I'm meeting Carrie and Jen for coffee afterwards. I probably won't be back much before eleven. See you later, love." Rose kissed Tom and left the room.

Cycling to the arena, she found the fitness room positively bulging with people, for many were snowbirds having recently returned from the warmth of Florida, Mexico, or Arizona. The class was as robust as ever. Rose adored the music they played, mostly retro sixties and seventies songs, all from her own era. Sometimes she bopped along to the music, oblivious to the exercise instructions.

By the end of the class, Rose was desperate for a cup of coffee. Saying goodbye to Julie, who couldn't join her for coffee, as she had a doctor's appointment in Goderich, Rose mounted her bicycle and rode to the coffee shop. Jen and Carrie were already inside and waiting for her.

"Hi there you two. When am I going to get you out to fitness class?"

They smiled and shook their heads, "Pole walking is enough for us."

Rose hadn't joined the pole walkers, although she kept meaning to go out with them. Maybe in the summer she would, but then maybe not. The croquet season started the end of May and that would be her main priority.

"So, Carrie and Jen, did you get your tickets for the Literary Festival?" Rose asked while sipping her steaming cup of coffee and munching on a Morning Glory muffin. They really were the best.

"Actually, Mike didn't want to go tonight, and the rest of the weekend is tied up with the family, so, no, we won't be going."

"Neither will I, although I really fancied the Romance Writers Books and Brunch. Never mind, maybe another year." Jen said.

Carrie and Jen both sat on the Town Hall Committee with Rose. She had got to know them quite well since joining the board a couple of years ago. That had been the same year that the murders had taken place when the lead singer of the band called The Berries had been found stabbed to death in what used to be the Town Hall jail. It had been a shocking introduction to the committee but had in a way united the members in adversity. This year they had been incredibly busy during the month of February with the Family Day Soups On followed by the Cabaret. However, March and April had been quiet months, which had enabled the committee to regroup and have more time to prepare for the busy summer ahead.

The women chatted amicably for an hour and then Rose said she had to go. Tom always made fun of the fact that she spent more time talking and having coffee with her friends than actually being at home with him. Rose always retorted that in the summer she had never seen him and had become one of those golf widows. They both laughed about their social lives, saying that they were busier in retirement than they ever had been when working.

Rose cycled home and was greeted by two ecstatic dogs. Tom was just about to take them out for a walk and had them attached to their leashes.

"Don't be too long darling as lunch will be ready shortly," Rose said and disappeared off into the kitchen to make a hasty meal with whatever bits she could find in the fridge. They would be eating out in the evening, so maybe scrambled eggs on toast might be sufficient for lunch, Rose thought, and busied herself with clearing the breakfast things off the table and laying it again for their lunch.

ABOUT THE AUTHOR

Over the past thirty years Judy has written twenty novellas, various collections of poetry and a number of plays. Judy wrote her first full length novel in 2013 and developed it into a series called the Rose Blair Murder Mysteries all set in the sleepy village of Bayfield on the beautiful shores of Lake Huron in Ontario, Canada.

Judy and her husband reside in Bayfield with their beloved dog Susie and cat Thomas and enjoy visits from their children and grandchildren.

After retiring Judy and her husband took on a new challenge in their lives. Purchasing land on the outskirts of Bayfield they have planted a six acre vineyard and are in the process of designing and building a boutique winery.

Life is beautiful and sweet. I feel so very blessed with all my wonderful family and friends who continually surround me with their love.